The
Harpy

ALSO BY MEGAN HUNTER

The End We Start From

The
Harpy

Megan Hunter

Grove Press
New York

First published in the UK in 2020 by Picador,
an imprint of Pan Macmillan

Printed in the United States of America
Published simultaneously in Canada

First Grove Atlantic hardcover edition: November 2020

Library of Congress Cataloging-in-Publication data is available for this title.

ISBN 978-0-8021-4816-2
eISBN 978-0-8021-4817-9

Grove Press
an imprint of Grove Atlantic
154 West 14th Street
New York, NY 10011

Distributed by Publishers Group West

groveatlantic.com

20 21 22 23 24 10 9 8 7 6 5 4 3 2 1

For Emma

Who, surprised and horrified by the fantastic tumult of her drives (for she was made to believe that a well-adjusted normal woman has a . . . divine composure), hasn't accused herself of being a monster?

HÉLÈNE CIXOUS, Laugh of the Medusa

Bird-bodied, girl-faced things they are; abominable their droppings, their hands are talons, their faces haggard with hunger insatiable

VIRGIL, Aeneid

It is the last time. He lies down, a warm night, his shirt pulled up, his head turned away. It is the kind of evening that used to make me want to fly through the sky, the kind that makes you believe it will never get dark.

Neighbours are having barbeques: the smell of the meat – sweet and homely – moves across his face. Downstairs our children are in their beds, dreaming through the hours, their doors closed, the late light blocked by their curtains.

We have agreed on a small nick, his upper thigh, a place that will be behind jeans, under shirts. A place of thick flesh, solid bone, almost no hair. A smooth place, waiting.

Jake is not squeamish: he is like a man expecting a tattoo. His hair is getting long, curling over the nape of his neck. His eyes are closed: not screwed shut, just closed, like a skilful child pretending to be asleep.

•

They were colleagues, then friends, and at first I suspected nothing. There were long emails, glimpses appearing on his phone, apparitions. The virgin blue of his notification light in the darkness. Nights where we couldn't watch TV, because she was calling. Nights I went to bed early, enjoyed the whole bed to myself.

If I went in there – to get something, or turn a light off – I heard his voice sounding different. Not romantic, or gentle, just on show. His *outside voice*, the one he used with postmen, salesmen, people from work. I thought that was a good sign.

•

I lift the razor up – I have sterilized it, carefully, watching YouTube instructions – and rest it against his skin. I press down, very gently, and then with slightly more force.

•

Jake's skin was one of the first things I noticed when we met. It was like the skin of a young boy – he was a young boy – someone milk-fed, comfort-raised. Someone who wore large, voluminous boxer shorts. Who slept silently, on his side. Who had a blond head of curls, like an angel. Even his eyelashes were curly. Tears used to get caught in them when we argued. On his stomach, his skin was hairless and as soft as a woman's. The first time we went to bed, I kissed it.

•

I confronted him once, late at night, in my pyjamas, leaning against the fridge.

Do you want to sleep with her? I asked him. *I think it's best if we're just really clear about this.*

He laughed. *I wish you'd get to know her,* he said. *She's—* He paused, the silence standing in for dullness, advanced age, sour breath.

She's married, he said, finally. He looked at me, almost kindly. We didn't touch.

•

I lift the razor and a fairy-tale drop of blood escapes from under the silver. The colours are the brightest I have ever seen: stark and cartoon-like, white skin and sea-blue shirt and dark red, rolling and seeking. He doesn't make a sound.

I

~

I wonder if people would believe me if I said I have never been a violent person. I have never held an animal's neck warm in my elbow and cricked the life from it. I have never been one of those women who dreams of smothering her children when they are naughty, who catches the image tracking through her mind like a fast-moving train.

I have never forced myself on anyone, reached into their clothes and tried to milk love from a body. None of that.

Even as a child, I remember the seeping feeling that guilt had, when I tipped my finger over an insect, and another one, and another one. I watched the universe blink, from life to death, flash over as they said a nuclear bomb would. I saw what my finger could do, and I stopped it.

~

1

It happened on a Friday, the boys in their last rhythm of the week, me trying to stay steady for them, a ship in dock, something you could hardly see the end of. I picked them up from school, administering snacks, absorbing shreds of their days, the wrappers from their sweets. It was almost midwinter: the sun was setting as we walked home, dying down against the playing field at the back of our house. Birds flew away from us, crayoned lines across the colours.

Back then, I was always hearing flocks of geese over our roof, feeling as if I lived on a marsh instead of at the edge of a small, rich town. I would close my eyes and feel it: the green ooze of the earth's water, rising through my skin.

~

If anyone ever finds out, I know what they will conclude: I am an awful person. I am an awful person, and they – the finder – are a good person. A kind, large-hearted, pleasant person. Attractive, with a nice smell. This person – this woman, perhaps – would never do the things that I have done. She would never even try.

~

2

The boys were happy that day; there were no dramas, no small children lying in the middle of the road.

When they were younger, I was constantly picking them up from the pavement, facing the possibility that I would be stuck on the journey for a minute more, an hour more. A week. The eldest, Paddy, never got over the birth of his brother, and when he was younger he raged daily, making it seem as though we would be stuck in that moment forever.

Just before I found out, I had started to feel that the children were creatures I'd released from a cage. They were suddenly free, agile beings, looping around me. Paddy, especially, had a new internal quiet that I had come to recognize as a self, thoughts that were beginning to form dense and mysterious places, whole worlds I would never know about.

That afternoon he was being kind to his little brother, his gentleness a relief like a blessing, Ted so keen at every moment to stay in his good light, the almost mystical clearness of it, like sunshine at the bottom of a swimming pool. They were collecting sticks, fir cones; Ted had rolled up the bottom of his school jumper, was placing them in the bunched material, his little fingers pink with cold.

Put your gloves on! After seven years the phrases had long become empty, but I still used them. It seemed odd, that I had to monitor the children's discomfort, rather than simply accepting that they did not care, that they maybe even liked the sensation: flesh turned to ice, numb and tingling.

As we walked past the field, the sun was burning to death, so low that we could almost look right at it. Ted clung to me, and it was terrifying, when you thought about it: a ball of fire so close to our home.

The house had, in recent years, started to seem like a personal friend of mine, something close to a lover, a surface that had absorbed so many hours of my life, my being soaked into its walls like smoke. I could easily imagine it winking at us as we walked towards it, its windows so obviously eyes, the closed, discreet straightness of its back-door mouth. Even though I had been there all day, I looked forward to feeling it again: the calm, automated warmth of central heating, the steady presence of its walls.

When we got in, the sun's orange light was moving to the house's edges, up the curtains, ebbing away. The boys collapsed onto the sofa, their hands already seeking a remote. I was always liberal about television; I don't know if I would have survived otherwise, without the children's thoughts separated from my own, peeled away and placed in a box. When Ted was a baby and Paddy a toddler, I used to put it on for hours in the afternoon, the little jingles joining my heartbeat, becoming part of me. Even years later, when I heard the music of the programmes Paddy liked back then, it seemed sinister. *You are a bad mother,* sang the talking monkeys, the purple giraffes. *You have fucked it aaaaaa-ll up.*

Paddy was always capable of watching, calmly and quietly, without getting bored or distracted. In the early days, it had given me time to feed Ted, those long sessions that newborns need, sucking and sucking, the regular rhythm of his little mouth, Paddy breathing slowly next to me, feeding on TV.

Now, after school, I spent my afternoons as a kind of waitress, and I didn't mind it. Maybe it reminded me of the times I did actual waitressing, and coffee-making, and floor-sweeping, for money. I liked those jobs, the simplicity of them, the way they made me feel so tired I became transparent, completely open to the world. Tiredness was different when nothing was expected of me: it was a pleasure, sliding into a leather booth after work with my colleagues. Drinking so much I could hardly see.

I made the boys' snacks with the skills I learned back then, laying the pieces of bread on the counter in rows, spreading the butter all at once. I remembered my old boss at the sandwich shop, telling me how the butter formed a barrier, so the fillings wouldn't leak. They were always very stressed, those bosses, and I floated under their feelings, blank-faced, lazy. I felt a bit like that now, delivering the sandwiches to the boys on the sofa; Jake was always telling me I shouldn't feed them there, that it would attract vermin. And he was right – I had started to hear scratching in the walls, or the floorboards: I could never figure out where it came from. I spread out cloths on the boys' laps, put the sandwiches down, told them not to drop crumbs.

I was going back into the kitchen when my phone rang. It made a kind of quiet bleating, easy to ignore, but I moved towards it with something like urgency, thinking of Jake, wondering what train he was on. I had become used to the worst-case scenario, the 7.15, the children already in bed, his supper under a plate, the house and me alone, waiting for him. But I still hoped for the best, for the 5.45, for his burst of outside-world energy, just as the bath was running, as the dish-washer needed to go on. *Daddy for bedtime*, I would grin at the boys when we heard the particular blast of the front door, and their cheeks would rise up with joy.

I say that I was thinking of Jake, and his train, when I heard the phone ring, but I know it is possible that I am only inserting that now, as a perfect contrast to what followed. I missed the call – it seemed to ring so briefly – and saw that it was an unknown number on the screen. A collection of numbers instead of a name always seemed hostile to me, the sign of people ringing for money or favours. I turned the phone over, reached into the fridge for a packet of chicken, switched the oven on. It started again, the lamb-like building of single high notes, so close to my hand now, no ignoring it. I turned it over, saw it was my voicemail, lifted it to my ear.

~

This is it: the last moment. The children are watching television. The sun has gone, the garden nothing but rectangular darkness at the back door. I look at myself: I look at her.

She turns the dial, the oven is on, back-lit as a theatre, a wave of hot breath. The phone, lifted. She doesn't know. She knows hardly anything. Her skin is clear, unlined: she is only midway through her thirties. Not beautiful. Not exceptional in any way. But she has this: her lack of knowledge, stretching from this moment into forever, hers.

~

3

After the beep at first there was nothing, then a deep intake of breath, like the noise someone makes before sighing. Then there were the words, less like words than atom-crushers, some scientific experiment altering the composition of the universe, the plastic-wrapped chicken I held in my hand, the cooker, the sink, the radio.

> *This is David Holmes. I am the husband of Vanessa*
> *Holmes. I thought you should know . . .*

A gulp here, or a swallow, something too guttural to hear over the phone, the inner, liquid workings of another person's body.

> *Your husband – Jake, Jake Stevenson – is sleeping with*
> *my wife. He is – I found out today. I thought you*
> *should know.*

He said that twice: he thought I should know. The way he said it – even with the splits in his voice, the way it was balancing, like an adolescent boy, between high and deep – it seemed significant. Well thought out, as though he knew that knowledge was important in a marriage, that it was correct. He was careful to use surnames, for everyone. To make it official. He had a serious, professor's voice, maybe that was it. I have always had a weakness for listening to academic men, for believing what they say. I trained in the art of this at one point.

And so when I heard him say those words, the first thing I did was nod, very quickly, and put the chicken down.

4

I imagined how a woman in a film would react, on receiving this news. She would shake: I held out my hand, to see if it was shaking. But my hands have always had a slight tremor. I watched my fingers, their individual movements, separate creatures twitching in the kitchen lights.

The TV continued in the next room, pulsing on regardless. When I was a child I was disappointed to realize that television would not keep me safe: I had thought of it as an intelligent presence, able to sense danger. But then I saw a police reconstruction of a murder, and the woman was dead on her sofa, the TV talking over her head.

Please can I have a drink, Mummy! We had taught the children to say please, but had not taught them to come into the kitchen and pour water from a plastic jug set at a low height. We had not done this, and yet we blamed them, rolled our eyes at each other whenever they called out to us, their servants. When I was alone it was easier to be a servant, to lose myself in this particular pattern of movement, from cupboard to sink, sink to hallway to their thirsty faces. People complain that women lose themselves to motherhood, but aren't so many of the things we do an attempt to lose ourselves? I never minded the practical aspects much: the fetching and carrying, the work of the hands.

I started the dinner. I could only make a few dishes, simple things mostly. I had a whole shelf of recipe books, like most people do, and I cooked from them, occasionally, in a new-year burst of good intentions, or a sudden inclination following a dream. But these recipes never stuck, however simple. This is what stuck: a chicken breast, sliced into sections, each part lowered into a bowl of seasoned flour. Even seasoning the flour felt fancy, the faith that salt and pepper would somehow cling to the white powder and make some difference to the taste of the chicken. Cooking always seemed mysterious to me, the art of the unseen.

As I sliced the chicken, I noticed that it had changed, the fibres of the meat altered, more granular, the skinless surface almost opalescent. *I am a woman whose husband is having an affair*, I said to myself in my head, as though these words would make some difference to reality. Then I said them out loud, wanting to taste the phrase under my tongue, to pass its particular rhythms through my lips. I said her name.

Vanessa. The first times I saw her: laughing at our Christmas party. A soft handshake at a work do, then later: straight backed, clapping. A neat suit jacket, her hair tucked behind her ears. Where did she buy those jackets? I imagined that she had a personal shopper, someone who presented her with racks of almost identical jackets, described their subtle differences of tailoring. *Vanessa Holmes*. A raised eyebrow, plucked to a wisp, the tail of a tiny animal.

I noticed that I felt sick; I noticed this as you would notice that a book has fallen from a shelf: impartially, at a distance. When I was offered pethidine in labour with Paddy, they said it wouldn't take away the pain, but it would make me care about it less. *You'll see it there*, said the midwife, *but it won't matter to you*. It appealed to me, this separate pain, but there was no time to take the drugs, as suddenly Paddy was coming, and the choice was gone.

After the chicken was cut I squeezed an entire lemon over the top, like my mother taught me to do. My mother didn't like cooking, but she knew certain things. She knew about clamping your fist down on the thick yellow skin, digging your nails in, squeezing tight. As I did it I noticed – apart again, from a small space away – how it made me feel, as though a cool wind was blowing through my chest. I squeezed harder, the juice falling into the sizzling pan, my teeth coming together, my jaw clenched. I kept doing it, feeling my face contorting into an ugly shape. When I had finished – when there was not one drop of lemon juice left in that fruit – I turned around to throw the skin away. Ted was there in the doorway watching me, his mouth hanging half open.

~

There is a trail of anger flowing through my bloodline, from my great-grandmother, to my grandmother, to my mother, to me. Perhaps it goes even further back too, to my great-great-grandmother, who had twelve children, three of whom died.

One of them, so the story goes, was left out in a pram until his face blistered over in the sun. This is a story I have known since childhood, but when I told it to my mother, she said that I had made it up. I am left with the mystery of this woman of many children; was she too busy to notice the baby in the pram? Did she forget?

~

5

It was the worst-case scenario: he was back past eight o'clock, the boys asleep, me wide awake, curled in Ted's bed, my arms around him for comfort. It is wrong to look to your children for comfort, I knew that. And yet I had so many moments like this: after a bad afternoon, a bad year, his body against mine, his sleep the most soothing rhythm I could imagine. I had sung Ted to sleep that night; he'd asked for it, even after Paddy clamped his hands over his ears and howled *Shut up!* Both boys, in fact, had lain down quietly in the end, and I had sung until my throat was sore and the phone message seemed abstract, only very distantly dangerous, like a firework alight in the sky.

I heard the scrape and accordion-like breath of the door, so familiar, Jake's steps, his bag going down on the chair beside the table. I didn't move. Jake called out, softly, from the bottom of the stairs. He might have thought I was still wrestling with the consciousnesses of our children, pushing them into the softness of sleep. Too often, he had come up just at the point when Ted's eyelids were drooping, and I'd had to start the whole process again. So he only called once. I heard him go into the kitchen, shut the door, put his dinner in the microwave.

I think my parents were liberal with television too, because all I saw when I imagined dramatic scenarios in my life were those in TV shows: certain episodes I'd seen over and over, that seemed to have greater texture than my own existence. I could not think of a way to confront Jake that did not feel scripted, stilted, too cheesy or *on the nose*. I could fling myself at him, pummel his chest with my fists, demand that he tell me everything. I could, carefully and without crying, cut every single one of his work shirts into shreds. I could—

Ted stirred, his arm surprisingly heavy and strong in his sleep, falling backwards like part of a sail turned by the wind. He moaned something indecipherable, made an attempt to stretch out on the whole bed. I was going to have to leave. I thought of creeping upstairs, to our room, pretending to be asleep, but the thought was too lonely, too cold somehow, as though I could already feel the emptiness of the sheets, the particular creak the bed would make when Jake eventually came up, found me with my eyes closed.

As I started down the stairs, I briefly considered acting as if I didn't know, but the precariousness of this was obvious – *she* would tell him. And at the thought of *her* – the name had become unbearable, suddenly – something changed. Something became untethered inside me, as I had often feared it would, one organ seeming to break free from the rest, left to float, uprooted, around my body.

For as long as I could remember, I'd had a terror of my own heart. As a ten-year-old, I insisted that it was missing beats, ended up with my flat chest covered in circular plastic suckers at the doctors. My heart, it was proclaimed, was healthy. At sixteen, wracked with exam stress, I was even given a heart monitor, a hidden plastic visitor meant to record the incidents I kept feeling, my heart fluctuating, squirrelling, trying to break free.

I had been given the all-clear that time too, and no longer felt I could mention the things my heart did, all of its dives, its inversions, its battle for release. I gripped the railing of the stairs, feeling wrongness squirm and flip somewhere unseen. By the time I was standing in front of Jake, I was sweating, breathing quickly: I hardly needed to say a thing.

6

Jake got me a glass of water, running the tap until it was cold, testing the temperature with his hand, so that the glass he gave me was slippery with wetness, its contents fresh and cool as though they were from a spring. I gulped the whole thing, gasping between swallows.

He kept his eyes on me: usually by this point he'd be moaning about the train, about the other commuters – *so packed, so bloody rude* – speaking with his mouth full, gesturing with his fork. But now he was placing the food into his mouth slowly, deliberately, watching me.

How was your day? he said instead, putting as much normality into the question as possible. Sometimes I thought this was the worst thing about being married: the way you get to know exactly what every tone means, every gesture, every single movement. Sometimes, even before this happened, I would long for a misunderstanding, to have no idea what he meant.

I put the glass down, pulled the sleeves of my cardigan over my hands. I let the silence be for a few seconds, feeling the innocence in it, the reality of our life, the thousands of days without this knowledge.

Jake, I spoke to – for a second I thought that I was going to forget his name, that this is what would save us, after all.

Forgetfulness, some boring name given to someone decades ago lost, slipping by, letting Jake get away with it.

David Holmes – there it was, words caught on a hook. *He told me – about you and Vanessa.*

I swallowed, looked up. Jake held his fork in mid-air. I had expected immediate remorse, his face crumpling with it – this would be new, in fact. I had never seen that before. But instead he looked angry, that old dog, the irritation creeping up his features. He shook his head.

Fucking wanker. He dropped his fork so that it fell on the plate, such a small, domestic noise. Nothing that the neighbours would notice. He scraped back his chair abruptly – they might have noticed that, the walls were thin – then walked around the kitchen leaning his neck back, cradling it in his own hands.

He seemed to have forgotten that I was there, feeling tiny now, at the table, my legs crossed, the panic subsided and replaced by the water I had drunk, its waves breaking inside me.

He carried on walking up and down, as though deciding something. He came towards me, his face different, younger somehow, new emotions, new skin, his knees down on the ground, his hands reaching up for mine.

Lucy. Lucy, please – it was – it's not—

He was trying not to speak in clichés, I could tell. Trying not to say all the things we'd both seen, a thousand times. All of those stupid, broken, fictional couples on television, not even able to find their own original language. And here we were.

Vanessa? I couldn't help it. Her name filled my mouth, sat on my tongue. *Vanessa?* That sound at the end, sibilance giving way to an open mouth, a gape.

She's so – you promised me. These words through my teeth, as though opening my mouth again would be a mistake.

I'm going to end it. Jake mumbled this into my hands, which I knew must smell of the moisturizer I rubbed on Paddy's eczema before bed, a bitter, chemical-rich tang.

I'm going to— He was crying now, and this was the thing that finally disgusted me, that made me jump from the chair.

I had seen my father cry once. They used to rip each other to scraps, my parents. *Domestic violence,* a therapist once called it. But we never talked about it like that. Even an hour later, Dad could be humming again, frying bacon for dinner, a roll-up at the side of his mouth. But that time, he was at the kitchen table with his hands over his face. And he was sobbing, loudly, nothing like a little boy or a woman. Like a man.

Sleep on the fucking sofa, I snarled at Jake, a rose bush, a tarantula, a creature endlessly thorned and sharp-toothed, something that could spring at any moment. The *fucking sofa*, kids in bed, husband crying on the kitchen floor – cliché after cliché – how did it happen? At that moment it was infinitely mysterious, the way we had ended up like everyone else. The mystery felt almost like God had as a child, in church – something barely present, endlessly unknown, never to be brought fully into the light.

~

When I was a child, there was a book – out of print now, expensive – about a unicorn who went into the sea and became a narwhal. The book had beautiful illustrations, dark blue seas, peach-pale evening skies. But the picture I remembered best was of the harpies: dark shadows, birds with women's faces, who came down to torture the unicorn, to make him suffer.

I asked my mother what a harpy was; she told me that they punish men, for the things they do.

~

7

The day afterwards, we stuck to the usual, and I was grateful for it, at first. Jake brought me a cup of tea, and I sipped it in bed, watching him interact with the children, watching his normality, his *smiles*. Paddy was talking to him intently about some rare species of shark – a goblin shark – and they spent time looking up images of the monstrous thing online, both of them in their pyjamas. Ted was under the covers with me, still half submerged in sleep, his eyes only just visible over the duvet.

They had a friend's birthday party that day, and we went together, sipped thin cups of coffee in the soft-play centre, chatted to the other parents about swimming clubs and the new teacher. Jake only spoke to other dads: I noticed that I felt an obscure gratitude for this, as though it was a gift to me, a bird with a mouse in its mouth. I felt a curiously strong urge to tell one of the other mums, to drag someone into the bathrooms with plywood dividers, like we were teenagers. I could have chosen Mary: she and her husband had sex on Saturday mornings, I knew that already. She let it slip during an otherwise typical comparative conversation about screen time, during which I felt I was minimizing my stats, and she was maximizing hers. *We only let them on Saturday mornings*, she'd said. *So we can have some time.*

Despite this confession, her revelations went no further. Nobody's ever did. I had tried being candid before, at book groups and PTA socials, and it never ended well. Once, drunk on prosecco and inadequately fed on sushi, I'd asked what contraception people used. The silence was acute.

We should be so lucky, someone joked, and laughed. Everyone laughed. End of conversation.

I wondered if they all secretly had coils, jagged, effective pieces of metal in their wombs. I kept considering one but couldn't face it, couldn't bear the thought of someone pushing their hand right inside me. After one difficult *natural* birth and one caesarean, I felt that my body had closed over for gynaecological intervention, forever. I'd recently psyched myself up for weeks to get a smear test only to have it cancelled as the nurse stared into me. *You're still bleeding*, she'd said, and it had sounded like an admonishment.

After the party, we all piled into the car in the industrial centre car park, a light drizzle falling outside. The boys were moaning in the back, comparing party bag spoils, wailing about any differences between them. Jake suggested – without looking at me – that we go to the supermarket, and I agreed, my voice almost lost in concrete. In the car, I closed my eyes so I could feel just how fast we were going, how much I was letting myself be carried on.

~

I knew I was meant to pity the unicorn, to feel his pain in my own skin.

Poor creature, *my mother always said, turning the page.*

But it was the bird-women I felt for. I couldn't stop imagining what it would be like: my wings filling with air, the whole world flattening beneath me.

~

8

The feelings didn't start all at once. They came slowly, gradually. We went to the supermarket, and I planned meals in my head, dishes that I would cook and serve to all of them, that Jake would insert into his mouth. Jake would sit there and chew my food and swallow it: I assessed this information for cracks, for gaps that I might slip through. It seemed very important that I could tolerate this exact thought: the meat tenderized by me, stirred by me, being chewed by him, digested by him, becoming part of his body.

I thought that I could tolerate it, but I noticed another feeling beginning in my belly button, or perhaps lower, in my C-section scar. The feeling spread over my abdomen, like a menstrual cramp, an early contraction. It tightened me up. When Jake came back towards me, pushing the trolley, I noticed that he was smiling, telling some joke to Ted, leaning close to the trolley, where Ted's bottom spilled around the child seat, his plump hands paling as they gripped tightly onto the handle.

The boys were hungry, having left most of the food at the party, and as we shopped they began to throw themselves around as though their muscles were failing, becoming loose beings, grabbing things from the shelves. Jake and I presented ourselves for duty, emergency workers at the same crisis, speaking sharply to our children, replacing chocolate bars in their places. Our lack of eye contact, of touch, counted for very little. As we had been for years, we were teammates now, classmates. We were learning – or unlearning – the same things.

I was startled by how much the new reality was like the old reality: how we could still buddy up and parcel out the duties so smoothly. Jake cooked that night, making burgers with Paddy, letting him flatten them with his fists. And we did bath time, as usual, Jake sitting beside the boys, containing their wildness in the water as I scurried around finding pyjamas, tidying bedrooms, setting out reading books. I wondered if we could continue like this forever, spend a lifetime never quite looking each other in the face.

~

Sometimes I question whether anyone can know what it's like before it happens. Marriage and motherhood are like death in this way, and others too: no one comes back unchanged.

Even now, it is hard to look at that woman (myself), at those boys (my sons), with anything like a clear lens. My sight is still coloured, infused by the blood we shared, by their journeys through my light-less body.

~

9

After dinner, while the boys played on the floor, Jake came and sat next to me. To this day, I think he was going to suggest that we watch a TV series or a film when the kids were in bed, as we had done almost every night since I was pregnant with Ted. I have often wondered what would have happened if we had done that. I can see that imaginary possibility – which surely exists in some other dimension – almost as clearly as I can see the actual events that have taken place.

I would have put my feet in Jake's lap: a true act of forgiveness. He would have allowed me to have the remote – the first of so many small allowances, over so many months – and we would have turned our faces to the fire of the screen, let it absolve us, a living presence, an endless alternative. One evening – not that evening, but on some night not too far away – he would have put his hands on my feet, the first touch, and we could have started again.

But as soon as the boys were asleep, I put myself to bed. I carried out my skincare routine, the adult version of childhood prayers, rubbing my face in precise circles, my own touch gentle on my cheeks. Before I turned off the light, I rubbed cream over my hands, an expensive product with all-organic ingredients blended to create the illusion of calm, the impression of the desire to sleep. *This could be a normal night*, I told myself. *I have done the usual things. I am sticking to a routine.*

I was not even close to sleep when I heard his footsteps; I was looping around a curve in my mind, falling down the slopes of a particular feeling. I tried to stay there, to feign sleep, make my breath as regular and slow as I could. But he sat on the edge of the bed, tilting the mattress sideways with his body.

It seemed to be up to me to put the bedside light on, but I didn't do it. At that moment, any movement felt like a capitulation, an agreement that he could be there.

What do you want?

This came out as more of a whisper than I intended, the lack of light lowering my voice naturally, making it seem more like a question than an accusation, a soft noise between us.

His shape changed in the darkness, a collection of rocks moving with geological slowness. He had his hand on his forehead, I thought, from what I could see from the edge of my vision. The image was fuzzy: he could easily have had his hand anywhere else.

Just as I was dragging my arm out from under the pillow, turning my weight on my side, his shape changed, came much closer, his hand stretching for the cord of the light. I moved my own hand forward as he did it, set on stopping him. One of my nails caught the underside of his forearm: there must have been a tiny jagged edge, no bigger than the end of a pin.

Shit! What was—? Put the light on.

I fumbled for it, the small click, light over us at last, Jake's head bent, examining his arm, eyes narrowed.

I moved forward instinctively, as I would move to the children when they had hurt themselves, to reassure, apply the soothing balm of motherliness. The scratch was superficial, pale pink, but there nonetheless. I moved to touch it, and Jake's whole body startled, as though he was being woken from a brief, deep sleep.

His voice was wounded, little-boy tender.

What did you do that for?

It was an accident, Jake. I couldn't see.

It was becoming difficult to speak again, I noticed. There was something in my throat preventing it, rising up like an Adam's apple, blocking the way. I wanted something from him, but if he said it, I thought I might actually vomit, right there on the bed. The blockage would come out, I imagined. The talk-stopper. I would not be able to stop screaming.

I came to talk to you, Jake was saying now. He was saying something else.

I'm sorry, Luce. I don't know how else to say it. I shouldn't have done it. It was just sex, I swear. So stupid.

I realized my hands were creeping up, past my neck, towards the sides of my head. I felt the softness of my hair, pushed it to one side. I put the flats of my fingers against my ears. Shook myself from side to side, felt the heaviness of my skull, this weight that I carried around, day after day.

No, no no, no, I seemed to be saying. I was the child now, my body curled and soft in my nightdress, my feet soles up, moist under the warmth of the covers. I clenched my teeth. A tantrum.

Please shut up. Get out. Single syllables were all that could get through, mangled, barely complete.

I just want to help you, he was saying, somewhere in the room. He was off the bed now. I could feel him, tall and oppressive, by the bookshelves or the dressing table. A shifting space, a ghost.

Help me? Help me?

The sensation – gathering needles, an eviscerating sting – was almost overwhelming. But I was still within it: it had not taken me over. Not yet. I heard him exhale, walk towards the door. I thought of a surfer on the biggest wave in the world, staying upright against a mountain of water. That is how I could be, surely. *Not getting carried away.*

But when he left, I felt it rush through every part of my body. I threw myself on the closed door as though it was his chest, hitting the wood again and again until my hands ached. I expected Jake to come back upstairs, but I heard nothing. I expected that I would pass out on the floor, but at some point I must have crawled back into bed, and fallen asleep.

~

Sometimes, as a child, I would get the book out just to look at the harpies, to trace the way the wings grew out of their backs, easy extensions of their shoulders, lifting into the air.

I wanted to know why their faces were like that: sunken, creased by hate. I wanted to ask my mother more questions, but the words dried in my mouth, sat sour under my tongue, unspoken.

~

10

The rest of the weekend passed in a haze of routine. I was struck by how easy it was to barely speak to Jake, let alone touch him. Sunday was slow, its minutes thick and draining, the children grumpy and unsettled by its end. But by Monday something had changed. We were quicker in our movements, it seemed, as though the backing track of our lives had been moved up tempo, into some other realm, a fast-forward reality.

The memory of Saturday night was still strong, raising my stomach as I spooned coffee into a glass jug, infusing the grounds with its flavour. I poured hot water from the kettle, seeing again the way Jake had looked at me, for a second, as though he had never seen me before. In that moment, we were strangers again. We had not slept beside each other, over and over, thousands of times. He had not watched me give birth to his children.

The Jake of Saturday was, it seemed, an entirely different man to the one who sat at the kitchen table in the Monday sun, his hair filled with light, flattened on one side from the sofa bed. He was making silly faces at the boys, getting Ted to eat an extra three bites of cereal. Paddy found him hilarious, was howling, rocking back and forth on his chair until Jake switched to serious mode, told him to stop rocking, to sit up straight.

I had always observed this as a kind of wonder: the way Jake knew how to pretend to be normal in front of the children. It was something my parents never managed; every dispute was aired completely openly, as though they had never been told that this was bad for children. As I grew up, I used to wonder whether, in fact, they had some liberal idea that children should be exposed to everything, for the strengthening of their minds or souls. Later on, I realized that there was no theory or plan at all: that was just the way they were.

There were some similarities between then and now, some taste of the past in the air. I remembered how energetic my parents often were, after an argument. How our house seemed to be on its own trajectory, moving more quickly than the rest of the planet, making me wonder how we were all still attached to the ground.

I'd always suspected that, after they made up, the arguments disappeared from their minds, dissolved as though they'd never taken place. But for me, the fights came back constantly: under doorways, through the paper of books I read, a weakening smell. To be around their aggression was one thing, but to *not* be around it was worse: jumping at noises, forever having strange fears, of fairground rides, loud building work, dogs.

Today, for us, there was no routine farewell, no kiss goodbye. Even Jake, the expert in normality, couldn't manage it. He waved instead, while turning around, no eye contact. From the door, I watched him take off with the boys, his hand wrapped around the school bags they refused to carry, his voice marshalling them to cross the road. He was wearing a thick coat, a knitted hat. Under his coat, a good jumper his mother had given him. Under that, a cotton shirt: off-white, blue stripes. Under that, I knew, was the scratch: even paler now, peach-coloured, the skin already beginning to close over it, to regrow.

Jake would have known the proper terms for the healing: he could name it exactly. He had a scientific mind, was a biologist by profession; he studied bees, would bring home the tiniest fragments of his work, facts dangled on sticks, things I could understand. Apparently, he told me once, the name Queen Bee is misleading: she doesn't control the hive, her sole function is to serve as the reproducer. But over this, she has almost perfect control.

~

At school, the teachers asked why I always drew her: the woman with wings, her hair long, her belly distended. Is she a bird, they asked me? Is she a witch? I shook my head, refused to tell them anything.

I never shared her with my friends, never named her in our games. I kept her inside me, at the edges of my vision, moving in and out of sight.

~

11

After they left, I felt my mind fall, its scattered attentions sinking into the watchfulness of empty rooms. It was in this house that I first started *working from home*, as in living from home, relocating my entire existence to these rented walls. I had lived in this town for most of my life — only leaving to go to university in its similarly privileged twin — and had never managed to own a piece of it. But here, in this house, I belonged, if only for a *fixed term*. Wasn't life temporary, anyway, I asked myself; wasn't permanence a fantasy? But I couldn't help but want it: a mirage of safety, the pretence that four walls could keep your life, could hold you present on the earth.

We were, in our earlier years, cavalier about owning a house, or too poor, or too afraid — depending on which story we told — until it was no longer possible. Jake's career progression had been modest, mine had been in reverse, and meanwhile the prices in our area had risen quickly, silently, like mould along the inside of a neglected jar. The only people who could buy here now were bankers, corporate lawyers, high-level employees of multinational pharmaceutical companies, people whose values seemed somehow at odds with their aesthetics, their Edwardian stained glass, wooden bookshelves filled with books from their days at university.

In these houses, most of the women stayed at home; their husbands were busy enough that they wanted a housekeeper, a nanny, a constant, hovering presence. The woman – the wife – could be all of these things, and she could *keep her hand in*, she could join the PTA.

I don't know why I thought I was any different; I was surely the same, with less money. Today, as on every other work day, I was writing *copy*: a manual for an industrial gluing device. When I was a teenager, I wanted to be a writer, imagined I would write something more meaningful than the sentence I had perfected today: *To avoid accidents lay the cables so that they will not cause any risk of stumbling.* But perhaps I could never have written anything as useful as this, anything that would prevent a death.

Pre-children, I found work at a university press, still within touching distance of intellectual life, of the PhD I had once abandoned. I moved between lines of dense, taut prose, seizing mistakes, making it perfect. I even stayed there when I had Paddy, submitting cringing apologies for every illness he had, every forced day off. I was surrounded by male colleagues working late, picking up speed, their sweat permeating the small office. Ambition was here, somewhere, I knew. But when I went freelance – after Ted was born, to be *more available* for the children – I was hired by whoever would have me: hotel brochures, private school prospectuses, company training materials. I told myself that I was seeing the world, that I was writing the world. Maybe I was.

But today I couldn't concentrate. I walked in and out of rooms without purpose, looking out of windows, trying to find something to see. I watched a mother crossing the road with her children, all colour drawn from her face into the street around her, the houses, her children's wide faces and bright clothes. As they moved across the street, she put her body in front, before theirs, the first thing that would be hit.

In the kitchen, I made a cup of tea, tried to drink it before it was cool enough, felt the scorch on the end of my tongue. I couldn't stop thinking of Vanessa: her quick glances, her self-possession, the way I'd seen her smiling at Jake. *Like a son*, I used to think. My stomach turned. I closed my eyes, tried to slow my breathing, but all I could see was the shape of Jake in the dark, the quickness of my movement towards him, the spectral outline of his scratch: like a drawn-on mouth, trying to speak.

12

Jake was late that night, and I knew it wasn't the trains. I had checked them online while the boys were in the bath, crouched on the loft stairs, the light from my phone a cool comfort in the twilight. My thumb streamed through the arrivals: every single one had a green tick beside it, running on time. These were just facts, I reminded myself, pieces of information: they weren't personal.

There was no text. There was nothing from him, the expectant blankness of my phone reminding me of evenings – early on – when I had waited for him to reply. The first days of mobiles, the elegant, longhand notification: *1 Message Received*. I would leave the phone in my room and go for baths for two or three hours, putting off the moment when I had to return to the screen. *Jake and I were practically children when we met*, I used to tell people. We were twenty, idealists, babies intent on saving the world. We didn't know what we were doing.

I got the boys out of the bath, lifting each of them high, rubbing their hair, pretending to be some kind of robot – *the drying robot!* – blowing raspberries in their necks. They went along with it, laughed at me, leaned back their heads and let me do it. Ted snuggled in my armpit after, wriggled with delight. But as Paddy brushed his teeth I saw him watching me, his eyes tipping down, something like suspicion making them narrow, his mouth full of toothpaste foam. He watched as I flipped the plug up, as I grabbed the bath mat, shaking it vigorously, scooped dirty socks from the floor with one hand while guiding the toothbrush back in Ted's mouth with the other.

Are you okay, Mummy?

For their sake, I tried to calm down. Surely there were plenty of explanations for lateness; accident, illness, mechanical failure. Terrorist attack. Or: Jake could have decided to go for a drink with a colleague. He had done that before. I watched a wave of my own ignorance gathering at the edge of my thoughts, low, like tsunamis seemed to be from a distance, threatening to overtake everything.

How, I wondered, had I believed him so many times, barely even listened, in fact, to his excuses? Often, I knew, I was relieved when he didn't come home. After a day of the children's bodies soaking into me, I wanted nothing more than quiet, bathwater, my own skin. I had always needed a lot of time alone; in this way, you could say I was unsuited to marriage from the start. But we were happy, for a long time: I knew we were. There were pictures of us from the day we got engaged, standing at the top of a hill. Our faces were so young they seemed to blend into the sky. We were squinting, disappearing, our grins almost erased by the sun.

As soon as Ted was asleep I gripped the padded bed rail, swung my legs over his heavy body. I went into the bathroom, stood in front of the full-length mirror. I could barely see myself; I pulled down the blinds, switched on the light. My dress was damp under my arms and lightly stained with the oil I had fried for dinner. My mascara was smudged across my cheek. I had to ask the question, at last: how did I compare? I knew what she looked like; this was not the question. I even knew what she smelled like; I had smelled it on Jake a few times, I realized now. Shower gel, laundry detergent. Something else, from deep inside her.

Vanessa. I gripped the sink, retched into the plughole. Horrifying, how plugholes are, when you look closely. Some kind of slime, a greenness, reaching. I knew it would never go away, no matter how many chemicals I poured in.

Just sex.

I gagged again, spitting into the sink, wiping my mouth. At that moment, I found it hard to envisage them – *Jake and Vanessa, Vanessa and Jake* – in anything other than the most pornographic set-ups. I found it almost impossible to see their faces. I could only, if I tried hard, see a graphic close-up of their sexual organs, one inserted into the other, a basic mechanism, the simplest of actions. Something had happened to my imagination: it had become X-rated, an adventure in the furthest corners of the Internet, a place where porn adverts stacked like origami paper, a hundred edges framing the place where a penis entered a woman's mouth and left it, over and over to eternity.

He was not back by ten. I had drunk half a bottle of wine by then, a strong red that tasted more bitter the more I drank. I had taken off my stained dress, found something black and shiny in the back of the wardrobe instead, pulling cloth in fists from the hangers, throwing T-shirts and skirts on the floor. I knew that, according to movie logic, I should have been emptying Jake's wardrobe, not my own. But that didn't appeal: I didn't want to touch any of his things. I didn't want to smell her again.

The top note – the perfumed, manufactured part, shampoo, maybe, or deodorant – had an earthy smell, more like a man's perfume, or something unisex. Something that suggested whisky and cigars and steaming pools of volcanic water plunged into after chopping logs. A man's good sweat on a tartan shirt, rubbed with fragrant leaves. A camping holiday, without kids. I could see her on this holiday, not me. I saw the way she would sit in the doorway of the tent, with some elegant copy of a classic novel, her legs crossed at the ankle. She would flick her hair, laugh as Jake said something. Under her skirt, under her leggings, she would be as tight as the day she was born. I saw Jake whispering in her ear, telling her how sweet she was, how good she tasted, how much better than me . . .

I had to move to stop myself thinking, had to start doing something. I put a load of washing on, even though there was nowhere to hang it, even though the house was already draped with clothes, filled with their dampness, not warm enough in the larger rooms, even with the heating on. *I should make a fire*, I thought, but I didn't know how. Jake had always done it. I swept up instead, moving quickly around the rooms in my short black dress, a diamanté embellishment between my breasts. I used to wear the dress to formal halls at Jake's old college, a cocktail dress, *very flattering*, skimming over my hips. Now it was pulled too high by some rearrangement of my flesh, the caesarean surgeon's knife, the trainee who had been learning how to cut. My breasts loomed out of the deep neckline, my full-cup bra visible. If I lowered my neck, I could bury my head in my own flesh. I wondered, briefly, if I could suffocate myself like this, if I pushed down for long enough, if I really made an effort.

I swept and swept, then got down on my hands and knees to scrub the dirty patches. Our kitchen floor was the most neglected part of our house, mopping often delayed by the busyness of our lives, which, now I looked from this perspective − on the floor, miniaturized, the kitchen a giant around me − were not busy at all. There was plenty of time, plenty of time for Jake to fuck me and fuck her, for months. We'd had great sex lately, both of us exhausted afterwards, muted, gazing at the ceiling. He had come from her, of course he had—

Another retch, onto the kitchen floor, a thin line of spit trailing to the ground. I sat back, propped myself against the cupboards. These were the ones where we kept the Tupperware, the dozens of plastic boxes without lids, with the wrong lids, a stacked confusion. I was always planning to organize them; I never did. The house and I had agreed, long ago, to ignore things like this: pockets of disarray, small, hidden places where chaos broke through.

I reached for my wine, winced as I swigged it. I had barely eaten for hours: a couple of cold fish fingers from Ted's plate, one piece so mangled that I suspected it had been in his mouth before mine.

Far away, in the next room, the door opened, slower, more tentative than usual. I nearly got up. I nearly combed my hair, splashed my face, ate a piece of chewing gum. I could have run upstairs, changed out of the dress, worn something sensible. But I did none of that. I stayed on the floor.

13

I gripped the glass in my hands: I wondered how much pressure it would take to shatter it. I imagined the blood mixing with the wine, which would suddenly seem thin in comparison, a pale watery red next to the density that would pour from the cuts. I had seen this before, I thought – I could see it in such detail – but I couldn't remember when.

Lucy?

Jake sounded sober, grown-up: I could hear his thick-soled leather shoes coming towards me. I had an urge to laugh. Was it possible I was married to this man, who was now returning to me, calling my name? Surely it was more likely that we had been pretending, all along.

He was in the doorway, his hand somewhere near his face. A pause.

Lucy? Luce? Are you okay?

He squinted down from his great height, as though I was a stranger, collapsed on the street, a vagrant, in need of rescue by a suited man.

Where have you been? I said to the floor, copying him, asking something I knew the answer to, just to hear the words coming out of my mouth, to make a sound. Maybe, I thought, we could do this forever, our relationship a series of non-communications, until the end of time. *Out*, he could have said, shrugging. Or *How are the boys?* But he didn't.

I've been with Vanessa. We – we just talked, Lucy. I told her it's over. That's it now.

Eleven o'clock. *Just talked?* There was too much time for that. There was time for sex, at least, but worse – much worse – there was endless time for tenderness, hugging, carefully worded good-byes. Suddenly, the porn visuals made no sense, were replaced by *romance*, gentleness, small moans into a neck or an ear.

Our house was small; there were only three paces between me and him, only a few seconds of me scrabbling up, flying at him as I had seen my mother fly at my father so many times, my fists closed against his shoulders, my eyes almost shut, only an indistinct darkness, someone yelling, someone else screaming.

Fuck you, Jake. Fucking bastard.

I could hear the words, but I couldn't tell where they were coming from. I could feel only a blur of fabric, limbs lifted and falling against each other, a clash, a cataclysm of familiarity. Jake grabbed my wrists, hissed under his breath:

Stop it. For God's sake, pull yourself together. Calm down. Christ.

I stared into his face, hoping to see what I was looking for: guilt, shame, the dismal music of a future darkened by his mistake, an eternal repentance. I breathed hard, said nothing as I looked. I had often wondered how many times you have to look at a face for it to become truly familiar; Jake's still eluded me, still had new angles to present, lost corners, inches that could not be memorized. I still couldn't see him, not really.

He looked down.

I'm sorry. I've said I'm sorry. I've done it. I've told her . . .

He still had my hands between his; I could feel the heat of his palms against the inside of my wrists, the veined part, the arm joining the hand just as he joined words together, put her name in his mouth, next to his teeth, his mouth that had been on hers, his tongue . . .

I creased up my face in a way I knew must have looked repulsive, my eyebrows lowering to my cheeks, my mouth drooping, collapsing. I let words come out.

It's disgusting. You disgust me.

I'm sorry. I mean it. I really am.

He was almost whining now, a curdled kind of sound. I could feel saliva building in my cheeks, tingling and rising to the surface, nausea starting up again. I thought of spitting in his face. Jake was breathing fast, his eyes clouded. *Maybe,* I thought, *he wants me to do it.* He wants to have to reach up and wipe me from his cheeks, off the lenses of his glasses. He wants to be in the right, even if only for a second. But just as I moved my mouth, he dropped my wrists, turned his head towards a noise.

I will never get a precise measurement of it: the exact length of time that Paddy – in his spaceship pyjamas, holding his old toy dog – stood on the stairs, listening to us, maybe even seeing us, seeing his father holding his mother back by the wrists. I only know what we did, once we knew, the way we became his parents, actors switching out of their roles, instantly, as though at a fire alarm, someone collapsed in the audience. I felt immediately sober, my dress too tight, the sourness of wine coating my teeth.

Why do you smell funny? Paddy asked, as we tucked him back in.

Why are you wearing that? He ran his fingers over the diamanté shape, stroked the black smoothness in the middle, his eyes heavy, fluttering. He was barely awake. Maybe in the morning, he would think it was all a dream.

Jake had left before me, as though he couldn't bear to watch, giving Paddy a quick peck on the head, calling out *Goodnight, sleep tight* from the doorway. When I got downstairs, he was sitting at the kitchen table. He was drinking whisky from a heavy glass, the top buttons of his wrinkled work shirt undone.

Perhaps, I thought, *this* was how my mother and father felt after one of their fights. There was nothing we could do to take it back. Nothing in human history that said you could make things un-happen, take them away from memory, away from the mind. I once heard about a drug that gives the recipient amnesia after a traumatic injury or event. But presumably no doctor would give it to Paddy, for having witnessed whatever he'd seen.

I went to sit next to Jake, tried unsuccessfully to pull my dress around my breasts, over my stomach and legs. I reached for my glass of wine from the counter, sniffed it, made a face.

That wine's been open for like two months, he said.

There was something in his eyes: amusement, I thought at first. His mouth was completely set, it was hard to tell. For the first time in years, I didn't know what he was feeling. I could not imagine a single one of his thoughts. Only his actions were clear now: the way he reached over his face with one huge hand, moved his glasses up, rubbed his eyes. His other hand fell loose, palm up on the table.

Without thinking much about it, I shifted my hand until it was next to Jake's, then over it, flattened against it. He was still covering his eyes with his left hand, the fingers close together, slightly cupped. I could see his breath, moving his shirt up and down. We held hands.

It started off as a squeeze, like when you assure someone you are still thinking of them in the cinema, or at an emotional moment at a wedding. But when I pressed on Jake's hand, he didn't press back. Maybe that's why I did it.

I carried on pressing, harder and harder, knowing my nails were digging in. Jake moved his fingers from his eyes; he looked at our hands, entwined on the table, their different tones blurring together. He breathed in sharply, once. He carried on looking, but he didn't move his hand away.

Only when I'd stopped, my face feeling hot, a little short of breath, did he speak.

That's what you want, isn't it, Lucy? To hurt me.

He was folding his lower lip into his mouth, his eyes were bright, moist, but it didn't feel like an accusation. It felt like a statement, one of his scientific proclamations, a simple observation based on the facts.

~

Am I a good woman? The rare prize the Bible talks about, precious
above jewels. I know I am not.

But I know other things too: how easy it is to leap from your life: as
easy as your first step, your first period, the first time you let a man
exist inside you, feel your body grip him, keep him in place.

~

14

For a few seconds after I woke up, I forgot it all. Without words, with only the sun-bleach of a peaceful mind, I knew that Jake was downstairs making tea, that soon they would all be on the bed, and we would talk about school and clubs and playdates that week, the boys yelling approval or hatred, lying down like puppies to have their tummies tickled.

In these few seconds Jake had not fucked anyone else: our world had not changed at all. I reached my hand across the bed, felt the coolness under the pillow next to mine. I remembered.

Last night, after Jake said it – *That's what you want, isn't it?* – he'd held out his hand again, showing me the nail marks, deep pink crescent moons, a pattern across his lifeline. The marks were clear, indisputable: it was deliberate, this time.

You can do it again. You want to.

You're drunk, I'd told him. *Go to bed.*

I'm not drunk. I've only had one whisky. He'd held his palm up again, like my dad used to, a wide thing to aim for.

Punch me, my father would say, when I was angry with him about some trivial thing. *You'll break your hand like that*, he'd say, moving my thumb to the right position.

Last night, I looked at Jake's skin, shining in the kitchen lights. There were so many details, so many pathways. I thought of all the times I had kissed his fingers, rubbed them against my own.

Look, he'd said, *I know how much I've hurt you. I'm so, so sorry, Lu. I don't know how else to say it.* A deep breath here, a gathering. *But you can – you can hurt me back.* He'd lowered his hand, but kept his eyes on me.

Why don't you just try it, see if it helps? He was almost pleading. *You can do it a few times,* he'd said. *How many? Three?*

He was smiling, very slightly, his eyes glazed, the muscles of his face tensed. It sounded like a joke. But somehow I knew – through the alcohol, the blur of his hands on my wrists, my fingers pressed down on his skin – that Jake was completely serious.

Three. I'd said it out loud, after he did. It made a kind of neat sense, something religious about its structure. *Father, Son and Holy Spirit,* Peter betrayed Jesus three times. A familiar number, for a good Christian girl like me. I remember being allowed to ring the bell, in church: *three times,* I was told.

Now, I shifted in bed, and my stomach lurched, threatened to rise up out of my throat. *Why should I be the one who feels sick?* The thought came to me as though spoken from above, or from a tiny microphone inside my head. Surely, I agreed with the voice, it should be Jake who was being emptied, who had a hand reaching inside him, pulling everything out. Or if not him, Vanessa, gripping her belly, crying out. Or both of them, separately, wailing, swearing. If there was anything that could be compared to the agony of childbirth – which neither of them had experienced – it was surely an upset stomach. Gastric flu. The body at war with itself, the illusion of comfort broken forever.

~

At university, I chose to study Classics, of course: I chose as much of it as I could.

Sometimes, when I was meant to be doing something else, I would look for pictures of her in the library.

Twisted face, claws instead of hands. A certain roundness in her cheeks, her eyes heavily hooded: even then, there was a thump of recognition.

Originally, I read, the harpy was not a monster at all. She signified storms, thunder. Just bad weather, nothing more.

~

15

Instead of helping Jake get the boys ready that morning, I stayed in bed.

I'm ill, I shouted down the stairs, and it was enough. Paddy and Ted both came to the door, one by one, to wave, not to kiss, so no germs were passed on. I heard the thuds and cracks and clanging of the three of them preparing to leave the house. Jake called out a goodbye, from the bottom of the stairs, but didn't come up. Maybe he's forgotten, I thought. Maybe he was drunk after all. But in the middle of the morning, there was a text.

I had been numbly watching old episodes of an American sitcom on my laptop, the simplicity of screen lives taunting me, their fresh faces, the blessed closure of every episode. My stomach washed and gurgled as I moved my hand over it, an underwater world, shifting beneath my skin.

I didn't read the text straight away. I saw Jake's name and turned the phone over. I looked back to the laptop, to a couple in a diner, arguing over coffee. Was anything that Jake said worth reading? I had the invalid's sense that bed was a place you could live in, that there was a possibility of permanence in this state, my body damp and receptive to itself, my mind stretched thin by boredom, light entertainment.

You can hurt me back. Three times — then we'll be
even?

Jake had always written his texts in full sentences, full words.
He signed off with a single kiss: always one, never two or three.
He was consistent in that way, I used to remind myself when
we were first together. He didn't — as I did — get carried away
in the realm of four or five kisses. He was always himself. Now,
there were no kisses, but there was something else, something
that seemed better: a promise, a plan. A way to make things
right.

~

As I got older, I moved closer and closer to her: BA, Masters, years of a PhD, narrowing, winnowing, until the harpy was my only subject.

I gathered the scraps I could. A man-killer. A monstrous form. Golden wings. Golden hair. Perfect body, the feet of a bird. A face made ugly by anger. Frightening. Seductive.

The more I read, the less clear I became. And yet: I needed to know everything, to work out the truth.

~

16

I got out of bed as soon as I'd read the text, pulled on some jeans and a jumper. I would go to the market, I decided. I would make something fresh and delicious for supper, something everyone would love. Recently, every meal had been boring, expected: the same thing on the same day. It used to be normal: my grandmother made fish every Friday, chops every Wednesday. But now, I knew our meals should express the world itself, be varied and fascinating, an adventure on the plate. My grandmother never liked too many herbs, or spicy food, was known to ask for a boiled egg, like a child. Her taste buds were grown in blandness, in the stodge and slurp of a childhood of overcooked vegetables, lumpen, inexpertly made pastry.

Her mother – my great-grandmother – couldn't cook at all. She was a suffragette. According to my mother, she set fire to a department store, then ran from the police across the rooftops of London. She barely cleaned, or cooked. She liked to read for the whole day, to lie around in her dressing gown until her children came home from school.

Lazy! my grandmother called her. *Self-indulgent.* In rebellion, she tried to be a perfect housewife, cooked her husband gluey meat stews and potatoes, scoured and disinfected, gave birth to child after child. When she used to comb my tangled hair, she would pull it; she would shout. She yelled and swore and banged the hairbrush on the sink in frustration, making the mirror shake.

I used to imagine her anger as a parasite that lived in her stomach, that passed through the wall of her womb to my mother, who passed it to me.

~

She became my days: all I did with my life, for years, was read about her, people rustling, light leaving the library around me.

The harpy rips out eyes, I read. She drags and burns and scrapes and mutilates. She is ordered to do these things by the gods, but she is not reluctant. She does it with gleaming eyes: cut, smother. Poison.

It should not have come as a surprise to anyone. It should not have been a shock.

~

It is the first time. I have cleaned the house, from the loft to the kitchen door. I have not dressed up, but I am wearing decent, neat clothes. I have brushed my hair.

●

I have left my bed behind: I have stripped it, put the sheets in the wash, fitted fresh linen, run my hand across the perfect plainness.

I have cooked one of Jake's favourite meals, a pasta sauce with aubergines, reduced for a long time, until the oil shimmers, gold leaf on deep red heat.

●

The boys are calm, in a good mood; after school I did not put them in front of the television. I have played games with them, card games and word games and games of the imagination: *You are a horse, Mummy, I am your daddy.*

When Jake comes home, I do not meet him at the door, with slippers. That would be too much. But I am in the kitchen, smiling, stirring a pot. His sons run to the door, their faces alert, their eyes happy.

●

I would like to say that I almost do not do it. That when I serve the meal, I look at Jake, and nearly give him our sauce, not reaching for the separate pot at the back of the stove. But that would be a lie. I give Jake his portion first, spooning on a large quantity of sauce, garnishing the dish with leaves of basil.

He is unsure, I can tell, of what has happened. Of why I am smiling, wearing an apron.

Feeling better? he asks me, aware of the boys listening, his fork lifting to his mouth, and I nod.

Much better, I say, lifting my glass of wine to my lips. Jake is hungry: he takes bite after bite, barely chewing, letting the soft pasta and vegetables slide down his throat.

I feel fine now, I say, lifting my fork, beginning to eat my own meal.

17

In the morning, the nausea did not arrive, as it had on other mornings. My stomach was clear and light, my whole body in comfort, wrapped in itself. But the smell of the house was unmistakable. I found Jake in the tiny downstairs toilet, his head hanging over the bowl, groaning and spitting.

I've been up all night, he said. *It must be—* He paused here to retch, and I backed away: I have always hated to see people vomit, even the children. But he was already at the dry heaving stage, it seemed. He sat back from the toilet, his head against the wall, his long legs halfway out of the door, almost touching my feet as I held it open. The smell was intolerable now, acidic and fermented, making me put my hand over my nose.

– must be that bug you had, he finished. *It's awful. I've been sick about ten times.*

Last year, during a particularly tedious spell of work, I had written an advice leaflet for an emetic. It had never occurred to me before that there was medicine for this. I had only ever heard the word *emetic* once before, in an elective literature seminar, referring to the prose style of a particular writer, a never-ceasing stream of words.

Care must be taken, some accompanying notes to the medicine had advised me, that people did not use the drug for the wrong reasons. These reasons were eating-disorder related, I surmised, rather than anything else. This was for girls who took *laxatives* and *emetics*, who wanted to clear themselves out, to flush themselves away.

Jake stood up, staggering slightly, holding onto the sink. I could feel the words rising through my chest, small bubbles, like something exciting, something to look forward to. Even with the smell in the bathroom, I didn't feel sick. My head felt extraordinarily clear, my perception tingling at the edges, as after lots of coffee or exercise. *I can tell him*, I felt at that moment, the rising again, my mouth opening to speak.

Jake, you know the pasta we ate last night? I gave you a separate one – I – I put something in the sauce.

I would not delay, soap-opera style: it was done. Another surge of energy, a pulsing in my fingers.

This is the first one – like we agreed? My voice was weaker now, fraying at the edges.

Jake was lifting his head from the sink, slowly. His hands were gripping its sides, his hair limp and damp across his forehead.

What? His eyes were narrowed. He breathed out a stream of acrid air, moving his head from side to side. *You did what?*

Shhh. The boys. I put a hand out, as though to touch him. He raised his head to look at me. I could see the emotions travelling over his face: there was something beautiful in it, like watching a shadow pass across a landscape from the window of a plane. He was repulsed, shocked, but then – the shadow moving, the shapes changed by sudden darkness – he was thinking something else. Now, I too had done something terrible. I would hate myself, wish I had never done it.

But I didn't. Not yet.

We should do something today, I said. *Go somewhere. We should
– we should go to the sea.*

Jake looked at me again, an exaggerated frown taking over
his features.

What? he said again. *I . . . I feel awful, Lucy. There's no way
I could drive anywhere.*

I'll drive. I'd had my licence since I was eighteen, but when
we'd had the children, Jake became the driver. I needed to be
in the back of the car, in the early days, sometimes lifting my
breast out of my clothes to feed them as they stayed strapped
in their seats. Even as they got older, sitting in the back listening
to stories or watching screens, the tradition had continued. I
was the one with the snack bag, handing out fruit, opening
windows if one child turned green.

But I could do it: I could drive. I had dreamed about the
ocean, I remembered now, waking in the night to the empty
wrinkled whiteness of the bed, thinking it was foam, the very
edge of the world. We needed it, the dream seemed to say: the
wordless confirmation of the beach, the vastness of water.

We should go today. It was the kind of decision that we used
to make together, when we were younger, when we had more
time, more faith in the power of relocation. We would wake
up on an empty day and decide to go to Norfolk, or Sussex,
or Kent. We would speed away, our hearts running with the
road, any morning tiredness ebbing into the sky.

But: Jake was white, could barely stand.

No. God no, he said, his hands at his temples. He looked
much older, suddenly, confused.

Maybe tomorrow, then?

I have to go back to bed. He turned, not towards the sofa, but
to the stairs, started climbing them slowly, holding onto the

handrail. I heard him greet Ted on the landing – *All right, mate?*
– could imagine him ruffling Ted's fluffy hair as he passed. A
small, sleepy voice:

Are you okay, Daddy? Are you poorly?

Hearing this, I could feel that something wanted to collapse
inside me. Something wanted to give up, to stop everything.
But I didn't let it. Jake was going up to our bed, I noted. He
felt entitled to this, now. He would lie in our bed, and feel his
weakness. He would know – as I had known for years, forever
– how easy it was for a body to be destroyed.

~

Whatever people might think, I am just like them. I always wanted to be good, to be right, to receive a pat on the head, a touch in the small of my back. Well done.

I never imagined that I would hurt a single person. When I first held those boys – my babies – I was afraid that I would drop them, swing them from a window, turn their prams over in the road. It seemed to be a miracle, that this didn't happen. That we made it through alive.

~

18

On the way to the sea, there was almost no traffic; Ted had just grown out of car sickness but we kept one window open anyway, the coolness passing over us, the leafless landscape clouding by. Jake was feeling better, had even put some music on; I wondered if he had chosen it deliberately, an album from the beginning of our relationship, from our early drives. I used to rest my legs on the dashboard, let my hand lie on his jeans. Now, our bodies seemed to be miles apart, glowing with the separateness of strangeness. I held the steering wheel tightly, peered over the wheel. I could tell Jake was nervous, tapping along with the music, occasionally out of time, taking sharp intakes of breath as I rounded a bend at speed, slowed too hard behind another car.

Today, Jake looked almost normal, some colour back in his skin, but in the night I couldn't stop seeing it: his whole body sickly, weakened. I had slept badly, waking at what felt like hourly intervals, as though by a newborn. But there was no one there: Jake had gone back to the sofa without me having to say anything. It was my own mind waking me up, the same pictures flashing through, fast as a flip book. In the deep, tangled space of 3 a.m., there was no triumph, no energy. My mind had become light, rootless, easily blown from one subject to the next, every one of them dangerous.

This morning I had put make-up on my face, covering the black circles under my eyes with a glossy beige paste. I had phoned the school, told them the boys were ill, the lie coming out easily, simply. I had never done this before, had never been able to cope with the anxiety of the transgression, the image of the teachers' faces, sensing an untruth. Now, it seemed like nothing. Even Jake had called in sick without complaining. He just nodded and did it straight away, mumbled a few words into his phone in another room.

When we arrived, the seaside village looked different, warped, somehow, rough at the edges. We had never been there in winter, and at first the boys were bewildered, slow-boned, reluctant to get out of the car. I remembered that feeling, the sense that the journey was sufficient without an arrival, all that time watching the world unfurl itself, accompanied by music.

Jake had grown up near the sea. He was healthier by the ocean, he always said, his breathing and sleeping easier. Something in the atmosphere made his hair even curlier, as though he was returning to his true self. Today, I craved the smell at the edge too, its sharpness, gulls circling above fish, snatching them as they flickered into sight. We seemed to need this rawness, the place where comprehensible life gave way to mystery, salt water, death. Perhaps, I found myself thinking, this would heal Jake, heal both of us. Make everything better.

We crunched across the gravel path that led to the beach, the boys running ahead, their feet hitting sand before ours did, sinking deeply. On the shore, the sun was bitterly bright, completely unobstructed; I could see for miles, further than I ever remembered being able to before. It reminded me of the first time I wore glasses, aged eleven or twelve, the way the world suddenly became clear, complicated, every tree with separate leaves, every distant person with their own particular features.

Jake played with Paddy, showing him how to skim stones, bending down at an angle, releasing flat shapes over the water. The waves were too big; the stones kept falling instead of skipping. I tried to get Ted interested in making a castle, but the wind blew sand in his eyes. He cried, buried his face in my chest, his hair flying upwards, teardrops raw on his cheeks. I rocked him from side to side, pressing my nose to his sweet-head smell, watching Jake and Paddy play their game against the sea, their bodies almost silhouettes in the glaring light.

We ate our picnic lunch in the dunes, the wind and sun less brutal here, facing the marshes instead of the churning ocean. This part of the coast was a nature reserve, a haven for rare birds and rodents, pure green stretches in sight of the nuclear dome. The boys were calmer away from the sand and waves, with food in their stomachs. They balanced along the wooden boardwalks across the marshes, their legs teetering above the waving grasses, their arms wide out for balance. It was parental perfection: they were free, but we could see them, could – if needed – swoop down at any moment.

I smiled at a silly wave Paddy was doing at us, sticking his bottom out, his hands flapping by his face. I saw Jake watching too, but he wasn't smiling. He hadn't eaten much, just a couple of crisps, a few bites of an apple before sailing it into the dunes.

How are you feeling now? I forced the words out slowly, continuing to watch Paddy.

Better. He pulled up a clump of sea-grass beside him, tossed it away.

The boys seemed to have invented a game now, Paddy in the lead, directing his little brother with his finger.

We're carrying on with it, aren't we? My voice was reedy against the sound of the sea, the yells of the boys.

Jake blew out his breath, tugged at the grass again.

Yes, he said quietly. The word crept across the sand with the wind.

Yes, he said again, louder this time, more convincing. *I think we should.* He turned to me, not smiling or frowning, his face entirely open, his gaze steady. I saw myself reflected in his eyes, miniaturized. Harmless.

There are so many different ways to make a family: to keep making it, day after day. And this was ours: the plan was real, had already begun, was as tangible as our hands in the sand, the small boys we had created from nothing. Trips away had always made our lives feel malleable, easy to change, a toy world, lit from above. In this place – with the sea behind us, the marshes in front, the landscape stretching to the horizon – things were, at last, wide and simple: a man and a woman, our legs folded under us, our children playing in front of our eyes.

II

~

I have never strangled an animal, but I have eaten dead ones, over and over and over again. I have wrapped my hands around a class-mate's arm, twisted, as though wringing out damp washing, watching redness spread underneath. I have read many books about a girl murderer, a child whose eyes were invisible in photographs, two pits I couldn't see the ends of.

I have stood in the kitchen with my face folding, my nose sharper, my brow lowered, my changing turned to the wall.

~

19

It was nearly Christmas; I knew the next one would have to wait. What we were doing had no place in the boys' cyclical sense of time, the reassurance of the same ornament coming out of the box, the same song being sung at school. There was no tradition for our actions, no precedent; we were making it up as we went along. Certain boundaries had been established: they would all be *surprises*, we had agreed, like the first. He wouldn't know what was coming.

I was saying no a lot, declining invitations to drinks, carol singing, book club socials. I spent most evenings by myself, pretending to work. I had some new hobbies, it seemed, interests that were nothing to do with my life, made no money, contributed negatively to the smooth running of our household. Jake was often home late, having texted me carefully – too carefully – with all the details of his train mishaps: signal failures, leaves, bodies on the line. I put the boys to bed as early as I could, went upstairs to my warmly lit desk, to the open mouth of a search engine.

My laptop was now my most intimate companion, a thin space containing so many places to slip to. One week, I looked at nothing but tornados, giant dark chimneys of air spinning around fields, followed by the camera, an eye that revealed its humanness every time it retreated, realizing it had gone too close. Every time, I willed it to keep going, to go straight through the swirling, smoke-grey mass, through the cows and chairs lifted in the air, right into the centre, where everything is calm. Occasionally, one of the children would wander in sleepily; I shut the laptop fast, before they could even glimpse what was on the screen.

I watched tsunamis, bodies of water that were able to bring down buildings, to lift and carry cars, sweep away a city like the wipe of a cloth. The website suggested other videos I might like: landslides, helicopter crashes, explosions. I clicked from one catastrophe to the next, soothed by their repetition, by the way terror unfolded across the smooth shapes of my bedroom. The images stopped – for a few minutes at a time – the racing of my mind, its skimming over the surface of my life, across the surface of the planet itself, unable to slow down. I had not felt such speed since my early twenties, learning forgotten languages, feeling their contours rise and open as I pressed them. Before my eyes, ancient symbols became moist, pliable: they gave themselves to me, gladly. But now my own pace scared me: I was barely in control, it seemed, lifting endlessly through columns of thought with no clear way to land.

I was always ashamed the next morning, as though I had spent the night looking at bad porn instead of witness accounts, live footage, shaking images, covered in screams. I could see that there were legitimate cravings for violence, and repugnant ones; watching news footage, at the time, was acceptable. Watching it five or ten years later was not. Reading true-crime books, listening to podcasts about mass murder: all fine. Watching a video of a man dragging his bleeding friend down the street, listening to the audio of a school gun attack, a plane going into a building, over and over again: these were signs of disturbance. And yet, I wasn't alone. Ten million views, twenty million, three hundred million views, said the pale grey text below the clips, the number sometimes scrolling upwards even while I watched.

On Christmas Eve, we were due to have our annual drinks party for neighbours and friends, featuring fairy lights, mistletoe, mulled wine, no one left sober. All year, it was my single gesture towards sociability, towards making friends of our school acquaintances, people we knew from choirs and sports clubs and taking out the bins. To not have it would show that something was wrong, I reasoned, during one sleepless night. It would make people ask what was happening.

We're not doing that this year, are we? Jake had said, when I'd brought it up casually one breakfast time, the garden winter-bare behind us, a weak, egg-white sun beginning to break through the clouds.

Why not? I'd replied, daring him to answer in front of the boys, to break their absorption in bowls of cereal, their thick morning breathing. Jake said nothing, his eyes shadowed from lack of sleep. Every morning, he staggered from the living room in boxers and a T-shirt, waving cheerily to the children as though it was normal.

I had tried not to think of last year's party. Or I had thought of it, deliberately, until the thought made me feel I was coiling inside, twisting like a swinging rope. Vanessa and David Holmes, both of them in elegant, timeless clothes, hovering by the tree like the elder statesmen of the party, at least ten years older than everyone else. David's message on my voicemail – left unanswered and whole, deleted automatically after seven days – had only just left my mind, and now there was this to remember. The awkward, last-minute invitation – Jake'd sent Vanessa a text, he told me – the obviousness of their difference from the rest of our guests.

They had seemed to find it quaint, the colourful paper cups, napkins instead of plates, people dropping food all over the carpet. One of the neighbours was wearing his cycling clothes. Another had brought a breastfeeding toddler who pulled up her mother's shirt whenever she felt like it, wrapping her body around, arranging the small strawberry of her mouth into position.

I had seen Vanessa's eyes moving over all of this: she had the quiet amusement of someone who is past certain things, has grown above them, like a tall tree. Perhaps, I thought, after all of her generation are dead, there will be no more like her, people who are able to look at everything so calmly, as though, just outside the door or ten thousand miles away, there isn't a tornado just beginning, roaring into life.

~

Nobody thinks they will become that woman until it happens. They walk down the street, knowing it will never be them.

They have no idea how it is: like the turning of a foot on a crack in the pavement, the slip of an ankle from the kerb, a falling, a single instant, the briefest action, changing it all.

~

20

I had ample time to make arrangements for the party; work was slow at this time of year, my days unnaturally clear, full of space. I could hover around the boys, drop them off and pick them up every day. This was the ideal, I'd supposed. As a child, my mother had rarely picked me up from school: she was too busy working. Sometimes, both of them went out in the evenings, putting me to bed without saying anything. Once, I'd woken up to a babysitter I had never seen before, a teenage boy, his long legs a sharp V on our sofa. I was embarrassed in my thin nightie, no pants, my hair tangled with sleep.

I would do things differently, I'd promised myself. I would be there. But so often, my children seemed restless, bored with my company, as though they'd rather I was someone else. And when there was no work, I was left like this, a *woman of leisure*, the house and I staring at each other through every empty hour. At least, I'd realized, the party would give me something to do.

On the day before Christmas Eve, I cycled to the shops to buy a few extra supplies. Paddy and Jake were at home, the television murmuring into dim rooms. Ted was in his child seat behind me, singing a long and complex song about death.

Some people die of canceeeer, he intoned, his little voice lifting as we went over a bump in the road. *And some die of . . . BUUUM!* This last word was delivered in a triumphant, tuneless boom. A couple turned as we passed them by: from the front, you couldn't see a child, so it looked, at first, as if I was singing these songs to myself.

Everything about the preparations reminded me of last year, of the strangeness of having one of Jake's colleagues at our Christmas drinks: he had never invited any of them before. But Vanessa lived in the same town, she was *local*. She had just arrived in Jake's department from a university in Scotland: he was being friendly, he was helping her *settle in*. These were the phrases he used, at the beginning, when the coffees and lunches and then evening drinks were happening. He had been perfectly transparent, open, in many ways back to his old self, the sweet-breathed, clean-underwear boy I'd met years ago.

In the supermarket, as I put the mulled wine in the basket, I remembered Vanessa's question last year: *This is lovely, Lucy. Did you make it yourself?*

I had explained to her – smiling, touching my hair – the triumphant sense of having, for years, successfully thrown a party that required nothing to be made, almost no preparation, barely any tidying up. The message was clear: I am a terrible hostess! And also: I am the best hostess, the one who has overcome all the shoddy manacles of domestic enslavement. I take little care, and everything turns out perfectly. Her lines, in response, were meant to be a generalized compliment, one that acknowledged all I had achieved without even trying.

I should have known right then: at the exact moment when I held the bone of self-deprecation out to her, dangled it in the air. This was an offering, an agreement between women that

she should, however falsely, take into her mouth. But she spat
it out.

Oh, she said, her mouth rising in the small way that conceals
repulsion. *Right*. The mouth again, the briefest nod of the head.
I made an excuse:

I've got to check on something . . .

And moved away, seeing as I did the way Vanessa turned to
her husband, pointed to a book on the shelf, one of Jake's. *The
Development of Superior Species Characteristics*, perhaps.

Such an interesting . . . I had walked away before I could hear
the rest of her sentence, poured myself another glass of mulled
wine in the kitchen, let its warmth flood through me like
pleasure.

Now, I asked Ted to help me get four packets of mince pies
down from the shelf, knowing that the assignment of a task would
lower the chances of a frenzied performance of lack, the unleashing
of animal instincts all over the shop floor. No matter if every
young child behaved like this: these explosions always carried a
sense of particular failure, of *personal* motherly insufficiency.

There were countries in the world, I had been told, where
they loved children, appreciated their very presence in restaurants, in shops and cafes. As soon as I heard that, I knew I didn't
live in one. Ever since giving birth, I had walked through a
tunnel of public expectation and disapproval, a place with
particular lighting, filters that showed up every possible fault. I
had become accustomed to the posture I needed to assume
within the tunnel: a certain straightness of back, an avoidance
of eye contact. As we packed our bags, I kept speaking to Ted,
keeping my eyes trained carefully on him, or the cashier. Looking
up was a mistake, I had learned: it invited comment.

I loaded the shopping into my basket, held Ted's hand as he

stepped delicately across the low wall of the supermarket, lifted him into his bike seat. As we cycled past the postbox I saw someone I recognized; I prepared to smile-and-cycle-on, perhaps to raise my hand from the handlebar in a quick greeting. But she called out my name, stepped forwards slightly towards the bike. Mary.

I stopped, balancing my legs on either side of the frame, Ted yelping in complaint behind me.

How are you? My heart was beating very quickly, I noticed: I resisted the urge to take my own pulse, to check for regularity.

We're good thanks, you? Mary rallied without pause, without a second to consider her answer. I did the same, my voice level as a bank clerk.

We're okay, same old, really, you know.

I had long stopped noticing the tendency to refer to ourselves in the first person plural, as though we – two women, on a windy side street – encompassed multitudes, our expansive beings filled with our husbands and children. But I noticed it now. I thought about it, as Mary gave me a brief update on each of her children, making their lives sound both challenging and worthy, as though they were international diplomats, rather than primary-school children.

So great to catch up. I was completely used to taking the bone into my mouth, however bad it tasted: I was a pro. I let a few seconds pass before I turned around to wince towards Ted, blaming his complaints for us having to leave. But he was now completely silent, sucking the strap of the bike seat, a look of severe concentration on his face.

Better get this stuff home, I said, trying again, tilting my head forwards this time, towards my basket full of shopping, as though it would melt in the freezing air.

Mary looked conflicted, pained, a near-stranger at a funeral.

*Lucy, you know you can talk to me, don't you? If there's anything
– anything wrong at all.*

So she knew. *Shit. Fuckity fuck.* I had noticed the swearing
in my head becoming very childish lately, as though I was
learning how to use the words all over again. Curses had begun
to spill out of my mouth, dribble-like, at ordinary moments,
loading washing into the machine, pulling hairs out of the drain.

Ah, yes. Everything's fine – but thanks. Thanks! The last few
words were loud, sharply pitched, yelled over my shoulder as I
pedalled away, the bike lurching to the side with the weight of
the shopping, Ted calling out in surprise.

As I cycled home I could feel the humiliation filling me,
moving my pedals forwards, driving me on. There was a flush,
the heat that everyone talks about, but then something else, a
deeper, slower removal of the self, a smooth sliding motion, like
a drawer pulled completely out. In its place: a gap, a nothing,
somewhere I had never been.

~

For a long time after university, I forgot all about the harpy. I buried my notebooks in boxes that were never unpacked, moved files to obscure places on my computer. It was easy, I thought, to get rid of her.

After all, so many obsessions pass like this, slide easily into oblivion. The boy bands whose faces used to cover my wall. A collection of porcelain pigs. The rows of stuffed animals: blank-eyed, certain solace.

None of them have come back. Only this.

~

21

As I tidied the living room, I felt her gaze over everything. I knew Vanessa would have noticed the teetering sub-Ikea furniture, guessed that the only good pieces — a large rug, a solid wooden table — were passed on by relatives who no longer needed them. She would have seen how dust had built up along the skirting boards, giving the house its own light grey fur, a lowering darkness. She would, without needing to think, believe that I was responsible. I had not cleaned the bathrooms while the children ate breakfast, as a mother at school told me she did.

Such a nice house, Vanessa had said to me last year, her fingers curled lightly around her ridged plastic cup, as though reluctant to touch it. Her nails were painted, a *French manicure*, white moons on dusty pink arcs. Her hair was *coiffed* — I could think of no other word to describe it — not fashionable but elegant nonetheless, a symmetrical loop around her features, a bow on the genetic gift of her face.

Something must be really wrong if he fucked an old woman. This would, surely, be what everyone was saying. But perhaps I should have been proud of Jake for so thoroughly failing to conform to the stereotype. At least she was not one of his graduate students, with a firm body and loose mind, someone I would have had to approach with an almost maternal scorn. She was so much older than either of us. She was of the generation that had it all, supposedly: the ones who were said to have taken everything for themselves, until there was nothing left.

When Vanessa had complimented the house, I had rushed to clarify, red-faced, holding a plate of mince pies: *It's only rented. Not ours. I wish!*

Who was I pretending to be when I spoke like that? *Stupid cunt.* I whispered this under my breath as I sprayed the glass coffee table, wiping fresh streaks across its surface. I didn't know who I was talking to but it felt good in my mouth anyway, a small wet kiss. *Cunt* was the best word for it, we had been told in a women's self-defence class at university, the most feminist choice.

Ancient, meaning sheath. We should have wanted this, apparently, to be a covering for a man's sword. At around the same time a man in a pub told me gender equality was impossible, as long as a man continued to be the active party in penetrative sex, the *doer*, the woman the *done to*. I'd tried telling him that surely a woman could just as actively *cover* a man, but he didn't look convinced. Even then, it had all felt pointless, word games that changed nothing.

Jake had taken the boys out to play football in the park while I got the house ready. We had sat together on the sofa a few nights ago as he systematically deleted Vanessa from his contacts. At that moment, it had seemed to mean something, the way the screen cleared so decisively, the way her information could simply disappear.

I hung a coloured bauble from the corner of the mantelpiece, seeing an image of Vanessa's profile picture in its colours, her face distorted, guppy-wide. Her *generous* mouth, big when she smiled, staggeringly large when she laughed. Good for—

I shook my head. *Disgusting.* I felt the sensation again: embarrassment, corrosive as acid, a sense of pitching, tipping into a forgotten emptiness. I would have no more children, but I remembered, now, exactly how pregnancy felt: like being taken over, *taken up*, willingly. I was – from the first positive test – happy to be inhabited, *possessed*, had loved having company at every second. There was someone to see the world with me, a silent, nudging companion, always there.

22

As people arrived at the party, I looked at each guest for signs of knowledge, every gesture open to interpretation. The way they reached for a glass, took off their coats. Their questions:

How are you all doing? Anything new? How was your term?

But these were normal questions, I told myself. These were the things people always said. I tried to stay busy, to focus on not burning myself as I lifted the mince pies out of the oven. Jake seemed completely at ease, at the centre of the living room, laughing with two of the men from his Thursday-night football team. He was wearing one of his best shirts, dark blue corduroy, his sleeves rolled up in the warmth from the fire.

Jake had thick, strong-looking forearms, always my favourite part of a man's body, although the hair on his arms was sparse and fair. My preference, not rationally, but from some other, storybook place, was for the hair to be thick and dark, hatched as a pencil sketch, like the deepest parts of a forest. I couldn't resist this sight, whenever I saw it, in a cafe or a playground or a train. Dark hair emerging from a shirtsleeve, moving towards a watch strap. It made me understand men who cut out parts of women in their minds, separating them, breasts, lips, legs, all floating free.

One of the men Jake was talking to – Antonio, father of

three − had this hair, visible at the end of his shirtsleeves, a thick softness covering his wrists. I offered them a mince pie, holding the plate forward until they had all taken one, still in their squat foil trays, too hot to be eaten. Antonio lifted his pie to his mouth, squinted, moved it away again, his eyes meeting mine. We knew each other a little better than most of the people here; there'd been a dinner party, years ago, where Antonio got drunk and started weeping, unable to stop. It was a strange, bright, summer night, dream-like, my hand on his arm, his cheeks wet with tears.

Maybe this was why I saw it, indisputably, as he looked at me. He knew. He was looking to see how I was coping. He was wondering, perhaps, how I was standing up in our living room, wearing a nice dark red dress. I was wearing heels: I had brushed my hair. I'd put on foundation, mascara, lipstick. At a party, these things, on a woman, are usually conspicuous only by their absence. Frankie, from down the road, for example, came wearing jeans and a T-shirt she'd spent the day gardening in, filled one corner of the kitchen with a distinct smell of sweat.

But Antonio could see that I had made this effort, that I was standing upright, holding a plate of mince pies. He was wondering how I was doing it. I excused myself, went towards the downstairs toilet. In there, I would be able to fan myself with my hands. If there were tears, they could be flushed out and disguised with cold water. I could press my hands to my throat, hold it in. By the door to the bathroom, I saw a group of women, mothers from the school, already waiting.

Much older, apparently. Like in her fifties! I know . . . if John ever . . .

I tried to turn on my heel − this was the expression, wasn't it, for a fast reversal, a quick getaway? But my heels were six inches high. There was nothing to do but wait, hold onto the wall, hope they didn't see me.

Why did they still have the party? I don't even know . . .

It was at this moment that Mary looked up: the words had already left her mouth, but she flattened her hand there anyway, as though to stop them getting too far. Her expression – of glee, passion, something close to arousal, her face pinking, her lips wide – moved downwards, a mime artist wiping a hand across their face, changing it entirely. All of the energy – the glow that had been making her hair shine, her eyes flicker – shifted through her features, lowering them in pity.

Lucy, we were just saying. We were just – how are you? How are you – doing?

She held out an arm, as though to wrap me in it. A mother – Mary had four – offering solace, a breast to cry on. Someone came out of the bathroom and, ignoring the queue, I went inside, calling out a reply as I pulled the door behind me.

I'm good, thanks – see you in a sec!

I let the toilet seat fall noisily, heard through the door as the group moved, muffled words, the tone of self-reproach ebbing away, top notes of scandal still echoing.

We all lived in our own version of parentworld, the place where nothing happened. We streamed TV to remind ourselves what it felt like to lead lives where things happened, where life could transform in one night. In our world, babies had happened, and they were something. But few of us had babies or even toddlers any more, and we spoke of those days with the kind of quiet reverence that elderly people use to speak about *the war*, our eyes misting over with the memory of the atmosphere, the breathy physicality, the murky blending of space and time.

Now most of us had careers that were still *on hold* or had

moved, somehow, to a forever part-time, lower-waged track. We were still many years away from the trickle of divorces that would begin just as our children became teenagers, their rebellions reminding us, in bodily, unavoidable forms, of worlds where things happened. For now, families were steady. In this place, most husbands had highly paid jobs, travelled a lot. Most wives, despite their multiple degrees, did all the school runs, counted the days until their men returned from Stockholm or Singapore. When something broke through – a disease, a death, a divorce – it was like a meteorite, something cosmic landing in our lives.

I thought I could remember a similar time from my childhood, a solid sameness, every day almost identical. Even then, things struck: once, in the early years of primary school, one of my friends' fathers shot himself in the head. He did it in his study. Somehow I knew the exact location; my mother must have told me. At school, there was hushed sympathy, *poor Vicky*, a sense of plunging tragedy. At home, there were dark streaks of anger, staining blurs of disbelief. *Selfish bastard*, someone said. I remember the kitchen tiles, and this phrase, the two things becoming one, the yellow curve of a tile's flowers suddenly selfish, its square shape a bastard.

Outside the bathroom door I could hear someone changing the music, putting on a Christmas album. Mary was asking loudly if they should reheat the mulled wine. She called my name, once, then stopped, interrupted by a murmur. I had brought my wine into the toilet with me; it was cool enough to glug now; I drained the cup. I peed, even though I didn't really need to, just to do something, to feel relief pass through my body. I stood up, looked into the mirror. If I splashed my face, my foundation would come off. My mascara would run.

I put my fingers under the cold water, and laid them under my eyes, the coolness calming, complete.

I realized that I was acting as though I had been crying. This is what I – and everyone else – had assumed I would be doing in here, away from them. But I felt more like taking my clothes off, having a shower, for hours and hours, coming out wrapped in a towel, my skin as soft and wrinkled as wet paper. By then, everyone would be gone.

23

When I emerged from the bathroom – maybe half an hour later
– it seemed to be a completely different party. The people that
were left – no Mary, I noted, and no Antonio – were all drunk.
Someone had turned the Christmas music off, put a nineties
playlist on, and now the rooms were draped with nostalgia, with
a wave of bittersweet, irretrievable emotion.

In the garden, there were groups smoking, talking with the
high-reaching voices of children. They had forgotten, maybe,
that they had babysitters to go back to, that in the middle of
the night their five-year-olds would climb into their beds with
hot cheeks. They thought they were still in the standing-around
part of their lives, when time had no particular boundaries, no
absolute restrictions.

Jake was not there. I scanned the groups over and over,
making sure, even though it was obvious. I didn't speak to
anyone; they were too drunk and loud to notice. I walked to
the bottom of the garden, sat down on the rotting picnic
bench, heard it creak beneath me. I took off my heels, felt
the grass moist through the feet of my tights. The field was
completely black in front of me, the sky infested with stars.
The house was only half-lit, its upstairs windows dark and
closed. From the wall beside the kitchen, steam blew in clouds

out of the vents, as though frustrated, waiting for it all to end.

There were some small noises behind me, something like a rodent at first, then unmistakable. Moans, words stuttered out. A regular, rhythmical rustling. I walked to the back of the shed, certain, in those three seconds, of what I would find. Somehow, he had smuggled her into our home, our garden, was fucking her metres away from where our children were sleeping. I was filled with a soaring rage, a mile-high surge of energy. I bent my hands over into tight arcs, tried to stand up as straight as I could. My mind moved faster than ever, skidding from thought to thought, no brakes, only an incredible speed, a readiness to pounce.

But the jumble of clothes behind the shed was nothing to do with us. Mary's silk dress was pulled up around her waist, moving in desultory waves as her husband struggled to hold onto her and thrust at the same time. He looked more like he was attempting a difficult DIY task than *making love*, but still they carried on, Mary's head buried in his neck, making small, obedient noises of pleasure.

I stumbled away, holding my hand over my mouth. It wasn't that funny, without anyone to share it with. But the urge was there nonetheless: gleeful, little-girl giddy. As I got near to the house I saw the dark outline of someone breaking free of the smoking groups, walking towards me.

What's so funny? It was Antonio, his hands in his jeans pockets, sleeves rolled up. I felt an involuntary tightening, a lifting inside; I lowered my eyes, as though this would hide it.

Nothing. I shook my head. *Just – don't go near the shed.*

Most people wouldn't let that lie, would keep asking until you told them the secret. But Antonio just shifted his eyebrows, pushed his lips out, as though he could guess what was going on, was vaguely impressed. He held out a packet of cigarettes and I took one, leaned forward for him to light it for me.

I didn't know you smoked.

I don't, I said, taking a deep drag.

He nodded, smiling, and we turned together, without speaking, away from the house, towards the sky. Our arms brushed in a friendly way, fellow spectators at the light show. *Could this be it?* I wondered. Another man, a friend of Jake's. A simple way to hurt him. A pleasurable one, probably. I imagined pulling Antonio to the side alley, where no one could see us, wrapping my hands around his neck. I could almost feel his fingers moving down my body, reaching inside me. When we moved back, we would be against the bin, the recycling bin, the blue one . . .

I let out a small laugh, without meaning to, some smoke coming with it, a splutter in the cold air.

What? He turned to me.

Nothing. I exhaled slowly. I could feel his stare, the prickle of his looking like a touch on my face.

You seem to be doing okay, he said. *After – after everything.*

So, he definitely knew. Everyone knew. I drew on my cigarette for a beat too long, filled my lungs with the chemical rush. Why was I the one who was looked at as damaged, faulty? Jake had been unfaithful, but somehow this reflected badly on me, I could tell. Just a housewife, really. Nothing achieved, no publications under my name. *Not worth staying faithful to.*

For the whole party, meanwhile, Jake had seemed relaxed, laughing with friends, moving his hair out of his eyes. I still thought – one last time – about reaching for Antonio. He would go along with it, I sensed. But Jake: what would he feel? He had never been jealous. I could imagine him shrugging, even smiling.

Good for you, Luce, he might say; he might not be hurt at all.

24

When Antonio and I got back to the house, people were starting to leave, drunkenness washing away the last of their politeness:

Where is Jake? Tell him to fuck off if you need to (this in a whisper). *Arsehole. Do the kids know?*

I couldn't help raising my eyebrows at this last question. *Oh yes*, I imagined saying. *We told little Paddy and Ted all about the way my husband started fucking his co-worker in hotels after work. Once, we said to them, Daddy had sex in a train toilet! Isn't that brilliant?*

Goodbye, I said instead, keeping my face tight and serene. *Take care, see you soon*; I played the gracious hostess well, seemed genuinely sad to see them go.

Mary was the last to leave; the sex had left her looking touched-out, pouchy, as though kept up all night by a teething baby. In fact, I had seen her in that state too: it was an accurate comparison, hair coming loose, clothes pulled around. After she left, I shut the door, turned the lights off, locked up, walking straight past piles of the party's activity, not stopping to clear away a single glass or half-eaten pie.

I went upstairs; I had told everyone this is where Jake was, *having a lie-down*. As I passed the bathroom I saw, through its unfrosted glass, the field fading into the night, barely distinguishable from the sky, a black strip running smoothly towards morning. If he was gone, I thought, I could bear it, could become as clear as this sight, moving forwards with simplicity, with poise.

In our room, the lights were off but Jake was still just visible, rolled on his side. I could tell he was awake: his breathing was inaudible, the room crackling with wakefulness.

Oh God.

I sank onto the bed, groaning.

Let's never have another one of those parties ever again, okay?

My voice sounded normal, calm. I knew I had said those words after other parties, on other years. Jake shifted around on the bed, still wearing his jeans and shirt, facing me. He was surprised, I imagined, to hear those words, that tone. No swearing, no accusations. Better still: I had referred to the future. Lately, the future had been banned. Our current reality was a lopsided version of mindfulness: no future, infinite present but also infinite past, filled with lies, half-truths, a dozen versions of the same story.

Really, he said. *Let's not. Ever. I couldn't take it any more.* His head was resting on his hands; in the near darkness his skin looked completely smooth, dully luminous, like the surface of a distant planet.

I saw Mary and Pete having sex behind the shed, I told him, and we laughed. We had not laughed together for a long time. We had not even come close. Jake put his arm out, as though he was going to rest it on my shoulder. I jerked back, a large, imprecise movement after all the mulled wine, the small, scattered dinner of canapés and sweets.

No. I shivered slightly, as though shaking him off another time.

There was a long silence, me sitting on the edge of the bed, my feet only just touching the floor, Jake quiet, still lying on his side. I realized I was waiting for him to go downstairs, to make up the sofa bed. I wanted to feel the room's emptiness again. I wanted to rest. I said nothing, heard the bed springs whining as he got up.

I saw you and Antonio in the garden, you know. He laughed, briefly. *What are you doing?*

The question seemed to have no answer, to have nothing to do with anything I could know, as though he had asked me the day the world would end, or whether it would rain in a month. I thought about all the eyes at the party, the way they'd looked at me. And here he was, hiding away from it all. Not even ashamed, it seemed at that moment. Safe and calm, wanting to put his hands on me.

I almost rose up, snarling, spitting with rage. But instead I looked straight at him.

I think maybe he fancies me. Maybe we'll . . .

There was another silence; it felt long, but was probably only a few seconds.

Fancies you? I don't think so, Luce. He's pretty happy with Jen.

Jen was a lithe blonde yoga enthusiast who had popped out their three children seemingly painlessly, without any noticeable change to her body. *Of course.*

You think I can't do what you did, is that it, Jake? You think I'm just going to stay here at home, snivelling, feeling sorry for myself?

Well, you got pretty good at it. He was reaching for the door now, leaving, just at the point when I wanted him to stay, when I wanted to rage at him, over and over again. Wanted to press my hands into him. Wanted to do something – anything – to get rid of what I was feeling now: a bodyful of bile, more, an amount that felt barely containable within one person, one skin. An amount that felt infinite, as though it could drain out of me, flood our house, lift our furniture, take over the world.

~

What is a harpy? This is the question I have asked myself, over and over.

Unnatural, she was called. Other names: Snatcher, the Stench, Whirlwind, Fleet-Foot, Storm-Swift. Ugly. Hungry. Foul.

~

25

For hours afterwards, I crept around the house, feeling completely awake. *What are you doing?* the house seemed to say, echoing Jake. But to this space, these walls, an answer came more easily. I ran my hand across countertops, felt the soft thickness of double-glazed glass. I knew it all so well.

I knew the one place you could hear the neighbours as though they were in the same room, every word of their conversations, strangely bland, as though they knew they were being overheard. I knew what it felt like in the boys' bedroom, the way the air changed when they were not there, the way it settled like dust, becoming part of every object in the room.

And in return, the house saw me as I was. Not as I had become: an average-looking woman in her thirties. Nothing like this.

I'm doing what we agreed, I whispered aloud. *I have to do something.*

It could not wait until after Christmas after all: this seemed to be a passing illusion now, an unreality of coloured lights, empty boxes wrapped in shining paper.

I went into the lounge as quietly as I could – Jake was a very light sleeper – the toes of my socks squeaking on the floorboards. I eased his phone from the coffee table where it lay, turned to aeroplane mode. He was so much more sensible than me, would never scroll through social media or emails in the middle of the night. He stirred, turning over, moving his mouth and making nonsense sounds, the room already thick with his sleep, the smell that men make in the night.

I tiptoed away, the phone beginning to sweat in my fist.

~

The harpy is an expert at stealing things.

She has always been dispatched to create disappearance: to make things not exist. Precious objects, people, the food from their plates, bites they were lifting to their mouths.

Like sudden wind, she comes down: she takes it all away.

~

It is the second time. Nearby, another, larger Christmas party is ending. There are fireworks, an amateur display, an uneven rhythm against the garden's bare branches. The quiet grass, the quiet field: the world is in its deepest sleep, but its people are awake, throwing fire into the sky, trying to light it up.

•

For a few minutes, I sit and watch the coloured flashes: I do nothing. I do not even attempt to enter the code on Jake's phone. I hold it in my hand, inanimate, like a large pebble, smoothed and worn by years in the ocean.

There is total darkness in the room, and then a flash of cascading light every few minutes, blanching the fridge, my legs, the window ledge with its small pots of herbs. There are cheers, somewhere, and the kind of wild, keening animal cry that teenagers make at a certain time of night.

Every time the light comes, it feels at first like a blessing, a benediction from God or space, and then like a warning, the totalizing light of disaster. *Christmas morning*, nearly.

I turn the phone over, its steady light so different from the fireworks, friendly, almost. There is a text from Jake's mother,

but I can only partially read it: the phone is still locked. I try
a series of numbers: his birthdate, Paddy's, Ted's. I try the date
of our wedding.

One attempt remaining, the phone informs me, something
humane about these words in the darkness, my only company.

09.10.84. My birthday: the phone gives way, all of its func-
tions laid out, available. For a few seconds more I do nothing,
weighing the moment, feeling its textures. I am tired; my eyes
are heavy. I think of climbing into bed, of being able to sleep,
if only for an hour or two. I could turn the phone off now,
return it to Jake's sleeping side.

But I think of his sleeping, of the satisfied childish calm of
it. Of the women at the party, Mary's face as she turned to me
on the street. Antonio: pity, not desire, I realize now, his features
softening towards me again in my mind's eye.

∙

I open the photos app, and for a long time there is nothing. Or
rather: there are the boys, our boys, the unfolding flowers of
their faces, the mysterious shortening of their legs, their reverse
growth, like time-lapse plants across the screen, moving backwards from school age to irresistible toddlerhood. Did we realize,
at the time, how beautiful they were? Do we realize now?

There are tears coming now, dropping over the phone's screen.
Waterproof, Jake had said when he first got it. *You can immerse it
up to ten metres deep.* And I'd imagined Jake as a diver in a perfect
Aegean sea, spinning downwards, the device cupped in his hands.

I wipe the moisture from the screen with my sleeve, breathe
outwards, shudderingly, into the bad weather of my own crying.
No photos. No evidence.

Then I see it: of course I do. A folder. *Work pictures*, it's called. There is one last shining moment of hope, when I imagine microscopic images of bees: their honey sacs, their small, furred, long-dead legs.

Instead: how to describe what I see? It is the end of my life, I think, the end of life like the end of the world in a children's book, a flatness you can fall into, a waterfall that encircles me. Here is Vanessa, and Vanessa, and Vanessa, and Jake, and Jake and Vanessa, and Jake, and Vanessa and Jake. She is naked, of course, or wearing just a bra, or just underwear. He is shirtless, and naked, and alone, and with her.

I breathe. I keep breathing, taking air into my body, releasing it. I try not to do it too fast, try not to hyperventilate. That would not help me now. I select one photo: they are both naked, they are kissing, their bodies one sordid body made whole, visible from the waist up, the camera held by Jake's arm above his head.

I click on the tiny box, the tiny arrow. I am shaking, but this makes no difference. The tiny box, the tiny arrow. Taking aim.

The list of options: email is the last, the original. I choose this one, complete the movement before I can stop myself: body memory, a mechanical gesture, as easy as riding a bike. I only need to enter one letter – f – and it appears: facultystaff@. So easy. *Send. Message sent.*

Undo, the phone offers me, kindly. *Undo.* But I do not undo anything. I let it go.

III

~

When everyone knows, surely they will say they saw it coming.

They will speak of the things I did: the time I laughed at a schoolmate's tights wrinkling around her knees, laughed and pointed and told others to laugh. Boyfriends I dumped or ignored. Words of hatred written in my diary.

We always knew she was like that, they will say, afraid of the truth. They knew nothing.

~

26

It was a beautiful early spring, the most delicate since the months after Ted was born. That year, I thought the world would never be beautiful again. The winter went on for years, an endless circling of sleepless nights, stagnant, swamped days. Baby-rearing, with the first child, had been a kind of somnolence, an amnesia in which I was happy to relent to the cow-self for months, to find pleasure in the cleaning of shit, in the flow of milk from my breasts. The second time, it was a combat zone.

My caesarean scar became infected, leaked pus until I was certain my body would split in two, exposing me. I found it difficult to accept that so many had seen my insides: the surgeon, and his assistant, and her assistant. They'd had a view of myself that I would never have, the exact, endlessly personal nature of my organs, their strange shapes, their unique arrangement.

At thirty, I presumed my life to be over, to have been taken over by the qualities that were always promised to arrive one day: pain, work, exhaustion. But the things of spring came, eventually – dimmed evenings and broken soil, a quickening smell – and I discovered that they were real. They could be called names, and the names would stick, would hold fast, as though there was no separation between the object and its sound. *Tree*, I would think, looking at a tree, and nod. It was true: this was a tree. It was a tree fringed with pink froth, a ridiculous sight, but real anyway, pieces of tree floating to the ground, a rosy snow. I even showed the baby, showed Ted, pointed and spoke for him: *Tree*. And in this way we carried on, continued to live. Maybe I would never be young again. But I was alive anyway. I was there.

This spring, years later, was similar, just as clear in its colours, its surprise. I had forgotten how much the house enjoyed it, being bathed in a warmer light, for longer. We had daffodils on the kitchen table, something comic in their familiarity, the droop of their heads, like grumpy children dressed by their mothers.

But Jake kept sneezing. He was at home much more now: allergic to most flowers, he would look at me accusingly every time he covered his mouth with his hand, let out an enormous noise.

Can you just stop buying them? he'd say, his voice muffled by the tissue pressed against his face. I would nod, empty out their sour water in the sink, fold their stems into their faces, carry them out to the garden bin. And the next day, I would buy them again.

This was how things were now; somehow, for the first time in our marriage, I had become the quiet, almost obedient wife, Jake the angry man, barking. He was suspended from work after the picture went out, pending an investigation. He'd got the first reply on Boxing Day, the reaction delayed by turkey and pudding, choirboys singing carols.

What the fuck is this, Jake?

You okay J? Is this a joke?

He'd read them out to me, his voice getting louder with each fragment, every movement of his thumb. It was almost a relief:

for the whole of Christmas Day I'd felt my mind becoming lighter than ever, its engine propelling my movements into overdrive, my heart threatening to split out of my chest.

As the boys had ripped open their toys, like starving people unwrapping bread, I'd provided a rapid, high-pitched commentary –

What is it, Ted? What's Father Christmas brought you? A mini-guitar? Amazing!

– while Jake filmed. He'd filmed even though we both knew how unsatisfying these videos were afterwards, when the gifts had long been abandoned, the preserved excitement of the day rendered distasteful, performative. My voice in these films was the worst representation of myself I could imagine: sickly sweet, wheedling, as though begging my sons to enjoy the toys we'd bought them.

I had tried to forget what I heard the night after the messages came. Stumbling exhausted to bed, using my hands to help me climb the stairs. For the first few seconds, I thought it was the children. The stifled, musical tones of crying in bed, mouth opening into damp cloth. I stopped, and listened. It was Jake, I realized: sobbing, making the same sound, over and over again.

Nothing had happened to Vanessa, he informed me one evening soon after. He was speaking through the bars of his fingers, his hands over his face, his rage so enormous that I feared – for the very first time since I'd met him – that he might hurt me, might pin me to the wall, as I'd seen my father do to my mother, bruising her wrists, leaving marks that she would cover the next day, pulling her sleeves over her hands.

It was my phone, he'd said. *My email address. It looked like – like I'd done it deliberately, to get back at V.*

V? I couldn't help myself. I'd never heard him call her that before. *V?*

He raised his head, and I saw it: what I thought – my many-layered outrage – counted for very little. It gave me no advantage; it carried no weight. Not any more.

Just to be clear, Jake said, as though he knew my thoughts. *This is over now, okay? No three times bollocks, nothing else. You've gone too far.* He almost laughed there, sending his eyes to the ceiling. *My God, Lucy. I could lose my job. Do you understand that? How are we going to pay the fucking rent?*

Here it comes, I thought. He was getting up from the sofa. I felt a shiver through my body, something in between total fear and a mild, barely-there excitement. But: *excitement*. I filed that away, to be examined later. *Is that how my mother felt?* He was coming towards me, I was stepping back.

Jake, I—

But he didn't hit me. He didn't touch me. He just walked past, into the kitchen, where I heard him turn the kettle on. Just like that: a click, such a normal, everyday gesture. The kettle would boil, and life would go on.

His life would go on. I was the one who had done the worst thing, it was agreed now. My sleep had reduced to half-hour slivers, places where I could not even reach a dream. Instead, I lay awake, trying to figure out how this had happened. In disbelief, I turned over its stages, its unfolding, its unfathomable narrative. I had become one of those women. The ones I'd read about, who have slipped away from the world, who exist on their own plane of scorn. My hands were no longer my own, I began to suspect. They belonged to someone else. *Mrs Stevenson*, perhaps. The woman who married Jake, who became a wife and mother, who would never be a real person again.

27

The text came in the middle of a routine evening, bath time in progress, Jake sitting beside, his eyes pink and cushioned with bags of fatigue. I noticed the absence where I would usually feel sympathy for him, a desire to touch his face gently, to kiss his eyes. In its place was nothing at first, and then the creeping pale of observation. I *saw* Jake, in incredible detail, every hair on his head, every pore on his skin. My vision was as clear as the camera on a nature programme; I could zoom as close as I wanted, without moving at all.

I was peeling a pair of Ted's underpants from the crotch of his joggers when the bleep came, the hopeful sound that so often – in reality – heralded a message from a group I was no longer in touch with, people who had forgotten to remove me from their list. Or: school requests; pleas for homemade cakes, for volunteers, women with time on their hands.

But this was different: unfamiliar numbers, a swirl of colour where a profile picture would have been. A painting.

> *This is David Holmes. I would like it if we could*
> *speak. Could you meet me?*

My first reaction was to tell Jake: this is what marriage does to you, makes you borderless, even in circumstances like ours, when we were barely speaking, let alone touching. We communicated only along the most basic lines: essential facts relating to the bodily health and safety of our children, to food or collection times or illnesses. Nothing else.

But I still turned to him, my phone in hand. As I moved, Paddy moved too, pouring a cup of old, freezing water that had been sitting by the side of the bath over his brother's shoulder. Ted let out a long scream, then began to sob. The boys had been arguing more than usual lately, had entered a phase where almost any daily fact – the colour of a cup, the order of bodies through a door – brought a sudden eruption of animosity.

Any idea of telling Jake was lost in Paddy and Ted's anger, in their small bodies bundled in towels warmed on a radiator, their careful sounding out of age-appropriate, nurturing reading material. There was no longer hour in our days, and none so full, our children climbing on us, closer and closer, as though trying to climb inside, to broach the divisions between our bodies.

Ted could only read a few words at a time, and soon got too tired to read at all, letting his head fall back against the pillow, his eyes closing briefly, opening again.

You read, Mummy.

For the first few sentences, Biff and Chip's latest adventure kept my mind in its words, in the glowing key, the sea monster that Ted traced lazily with the tips of his fingers. But before long I found that I could both read and think, that my eyes and mouth could easily work independently, leaving my mind free to return to the message on my phone.

What possible reason could David Holmes have for wanting to meet me? I tried to remember what he looked like, but could only think of disparate details: a brown beard, flecked with white. Narrow, pale eyes – or perhaps he had only been squinting in the light. He was an academic too, Jake had told me, the same field as him and Vanessa, a full professor at a more prestigious university than theirs. It was coming back to me now: his air of self-satisfaction at our Christmas party, at some departmental drinks thing, the sense that anything he experienced in these places could only be a passing amusement, a triviality moving across the depths of his life.

Ted yawned, and I let myself lean over and kiss his cheek, smell the musty goodness that collected under his hair, behind his ears.

Goodnight, my sweet one. Another kiss on his forehead: that was enough, I told myself. I kissed my children too much, I feared. I needed to limit it, to let them be.

As I left the room, I lifted my phone from my back pocket. I would delete the message before there was any risk of Jake seeing it and getting angry. It would be gone, not-happening just as quickly as the email I sent had happened; momentous decisions, whole lives altered by a tap, something barely more than a twitch.

I went straight to the kitchen, bathed myself in the cool beam of the fridge light. Upstairs, I could hear Jake reading to Paddy in our bedroom, his voice a single, steady noise. I reached in for a bowl covered by a plate, something else wrapped in clingfilm. Lately, I'd been having an extra supper, leftovers, scraps eaten standing up, without cutlery, taste after taste pushed into my mouth.

This was a new kind of hunger, the kind that made me hold a wedge of cheese in my hands and chew its sides, like an apple. I went through every bowl of leftovers in the fridge, spooning whole cresting waves of tuna mayonnaise straight down my throat. Just as my mind had quickened, so had my mouth, it seemed, my neck, my entire digestive system. I was always empty, these days, a completely open space, waiting to be filled.

~

As a child, I once made the mistake of telling someone. Wings, I mentioned. A woman.

Ah, the other person said, their voice only lightly mocking. A guardian angel!

On the news one day: a skeleton with wings. Proof, people said. Of angels, or something else. But it turned out to be butchery, rather than miracle. Chickens, fingers working in a dark shed, making the dead into something else, trying to make them rise.

~

28

It was Paddy's birthday in a few weeks, towering up against me, despite everything, a distant monument, its details hidden from view. A big party would be difficult to afford, but seemed unavoidable; how else would we keep him happy, prevent him from being an outcast? I'd sent the invitations before the end of term, hoping the Easter holidays would mean that most of them couldn't come. It had become normal to invite the whole class, at least thirty children, to hire a hall, an entertainer. Enjoyment did not seem to be the purpose of these events; children were often skittish and anxious, parents exhausted at best, traumatized at worst, handing out recycled-paper treat bags with shaking hands.

I spent a lot of time online in a cafe by the river, pretending to be working and instead shopping for pirate-themed party items. Cups and straws and pencils and pots of bubbles and tablecloths and balloons and miniature water guns and candles and tiny yo-yos, each with a different pirate image stickered on the outside. I roamed over the Internet, selecting and eliminating options faster, more efficiently than I ever had been able to do before: I could feel the energy building up behind my eyes, a sugary power, a vertical ascent.

Sometimes, I could think of nothing else. At night, I began

to see parrots in my dreams, huge ships with dragon prows, a soft rain of chocolate gold coins. During the day, I was getting very little work done; clients were beginning to send terse emails, scrapings of politeness meant as weapons, certain phrases chosen to wound.

We are disappointed that . . . We would expect . . . We hoped . . .

Always *we,* even from clients who had previously used *I.* The wounding was easier, I surmised, if done from a point of to-getherness. I could feel work slipping from my fingers, but felt unable to stop it: my mind was too fast for it now, it seemed. It could only skim above each task, picking up the briefest of facts.

Despite this, life continued, a new version of normal, a mode of being we adjusted to quickly: I still picked the boys up from school every day, even though Jake was at home, filling the lounge with coffee cups and the wrappers from cereal bars, headphones on, typing, his laptop resting on his knees. Working, I supposed.

I still cooked all the meals, loaded and unloaded the washing machine, the dishwasher, texted the parents of the boys' friends, arranged their after-school clubs, their haircuts and playdates and new shoes and eye tests. Some things fell by the wayside: the house was often untidy, neglected. Looking at me with scorn. But I went out to work: I came back to more work. I was being good.

And in this state of mind there was a new clarity too, as though my mind had been refreshed, its speed becoming some-thing sharper, my perceptions cleansed of the unnecessary. For years, when Jake had taken the children out at the weekends – to the park, maybe, or swimming – I had been convinced that one of them would die. This would be my reward for asking for time alone, for preferring it, however briefly, to the company of my family. *Selfish mothers don't deserve their children.* Somewhere, somehow, I had heard this, or felt it, ingested it in cereal perhaps, taking the message like fortification, like the dawn: something completely natural, entirely inevitable.

Then one day, as easily as it appeared, the message was gone. As the boys left the house, on their little bikes, I did not imagine the moment they would fall from them, their skulls cracking open on the pavement. I did not picture the time when Jake would look away from Ted in the swimming pool, just for a second, the lifeguard distracted, the dark shape of a small body disappearing under the water.

I could see it clearly, at last: the children would, almost certainly, be fine. And if they weren't, *it wouldn't be my fault.* This must, I realized, be what normal mothers feel. All the ones who are *very happy*, with their tasteful clothes and missionary-position weekly sex. Their stylish furnishings, the ease with which they let their souls go, let them pass, wordlessly, on to the next generation. All those mothers who no longer wanted anything for themselves, but sobbed at their daughter's clarinet concert and their son's graduation, their tears truly pride and not some concealed mourning (as mine would have been) for their lost selves, the energy that now belonged elsewhere.

I had even stopped checking Jake's phone. Ever since I sent the email, I had been sliding it from under his pillow as he slept, entering my birthday, looking for her name, for any new photos. But there was never anything I hadn't seen before: I learned to see the phone and ignore it, to let the screen keep its own sleep, its glinting blandness.

~

The harpy has never had children, it seems. Has never bought or rented a house, chosen cushion covers or selected a carpet from a choice of thousands.

She can sleep on the wing, her own body her refuge, her nails curled, ready to strike.

~

29

One afternoon, I got back earlier than usual: I had decided to put something in the oven before I collected the boys in the car, took them to their weekly swimming lesson. Lately, I'd only been making the simplest of meals again: piles of pasta, oven pizzas, oven chips, soups from tins. But today I had a leg of lamb, something I could cook slowly and serve with potatoes, with steamed vegetables. I was the one making amends now. Giving Jake something to be grateful for.

When I arrived, he was not on the sofa, the place he seemed to live nowadays, lying with his legs up in the evenings, watching television, programmes about space, about aliens, humans with very slightly altered faces. He had taken the house over: it was loyal to him now, I sensed, rather than to me. It smelled like him, even when he wasn't there. But today, when I went into the lounge, the sofa was plain and silent, looking oddly defeated without him, its cushions still dented by the place he'd sat for so long.

I wandered through to the kitchen, expecting to see him there, hovering by the kettle as he so often did, like the house-mates I'd lived with at university, one reclusive boy who I only ever saw at the kettle, making coffee or noodles, running his hands through his oily hair. But Jake was not there either. I

walked up the stairs, picking up items belonging to Paddy and
Ted as I went, two jumpers, a sock, pieces of an abandoned
puzzle.

Jake? I called up the stairs.

He was in the bathroom, with a tin of white paint and wide
brush, covering over a scribble Ted had done with a crayon
years ago.

Hi. He turned around briefly, then back to the wall.
Unusually, he was wearing jeans, old ones he only ever wore
around the house, loose around his bottom, pulled in with a
belt at his waist. A threadbare T-shirt: a band he used to like
fifteen years ago.

Thought I'd better keep busy, he said, still looking at the wall,
dabbing an already-pristine corner with the brush. He breathed
out slowly. *Still weeks until the hearing.*

He emphasized the last two words, slanting his voice into
a mocking tone. He'd already told me that he'd say his finger
slipped, sent the email by mistake. He wouldn't bring me into
it. If − when − he went back to work, he promised me, there
would be no more Vanessa. He'd resign from the working groups
and committees they'd shared, avoid her in the corridor.

Listen, Jake − I was twisting my hands, looking for words I
hadn't already said to him. Not *sorry*, which seemed to have
been said so many times − by both of us − that it had lost any
meaning, was now a kind of joke, provoking derisive laughter
every time.

Thank you − I went with this − *I don't know if I've said that.
Thank you, for keeping me − for owning up to it.*

Owning up?

I had managed to say the wrong thing, after all.

I didn't mean − I just wanted to say. Thanks.

Owning up, Jake said again, moving his head from side to side, as though he was weighing this phrase, judging its merits.

That's not quite right, is it, Luce?

He put the brush down, went to the sink to wash his hands. There were small flecks of white paint on his jeans, on his forearms, on his face. He walked towards me, and without thinking, I reached up a hand to wipe some paint from his cheek.

Very fast, he stopped my hand in mid-movement, held it in the air. Without meeting my eyes, he kissed me, harder and harder, his tongue in my mouth, the kind of kisses that are not asking for a response. He began to push me backwards, gently, and then with more force, his arm around my back, my legs moving with his.

Where usually there would be an opening, slow or fast, gentle or sharp, there was nothing. I felt nothing, could hardly sense his hands as they pushed my top up, grabbed one breast roughly. Jake had never touched me like this before: as though I was just a body.

I lay down on the landing carpet as he fumbled with his belt above me. He kissed me again, slightly more tenderly, looked in my eyes for the first time, as though checking. I nodded. Surely, I thought, this was the least I could do.

As Jake moved above me, I saw a poster on the wall, an old one, from his flat at university. I remembered the first time we ever had sex, something awkward about it, before the passion had built up. There was a full moon that night; I thought of the way we'd taken our clothes off and let the pale light shine on our bodies, the way we'd felt new: to each other, to the world.

30

I was going to collect the boys from school, take them to their swimming lesson, like this, with soreness between my thighs. I would stand by the gates and talk about the new playground equipment, question if they could smell it on me: I wondered how many people had collected their children from school with sex on their hands, drying in their under-wear. Rearranging their clothes under their jackets.

Paddy and Ted came out exhausted, hungry. I had forgotten to bring snacks; we had to go to the shop, where a tied-up dog barked loudly, scaring Ted. I knelt down on the hard pavement, took my son's uniformed body in my arms. He smelled of school, diluted urine accented with cooked meat and something like cabbage. He didn't stop crying until the dog was led away, still barking, by its owner. Feeling Ted's small arms on my waist, I thought of Jake, of his fingers pressed blankly inside me, as though he'd forgotten how I liked to be touched. When Ted buried his damp face in my neck, I wondered if he could sense what happened there, could smell the maleness, his own daddy.

It's only a dog! Don't be such a baby-waby, Teddy bear, Paddy yelled, his face creased by spite, flecks of wetness landing on his coat.

Ted bawled even louder at this, threw back his head to the

clouds, opened his mouth wide. Passers-by glanced down at us, at the noise.

Shut − be quiet, Paddy. For God's sake, he's really upset. I found an old tissue in my pocket, padded it across Ted's cheeks, tried to absorb the tears before they fell. I could have left the boys in the car, but I knew the looks I'd get for that.

On the drive to the swimming pool − the traffic bad, rain beginning to spatter on the windscreen − Paddy kicked the back of my seat with the hard tips of his school shoes. They were sturdy boots, a good-quality pair we'd chosen together one Saturday, Paddy stomping proudly across the shop floor.

Now, the kicks kept coming, a steady beat, starting up again after every time I told him to stop, my voice filled with more anger each time, becoming strained then broken, torn-sounding.

You're horrible, Mum, he shouted eventually, meeting my anger with his own, landing an extra-hard kick at the base of my spine. I cried out, pain moving down my back. Deep inside me, the ache of Jake's presence pulsed on, a reprimand. Paddy was right, I sensed. He knew what I was.

They were both quiet for a few minutes, hushed into dulled daydreams by the world rising and falling at the windows, the steady lull of the engine under their bodies. It was when the snacks ran out that the fighting began, dark scratches of noise across silence, yells that I countered with my own.

He called me a stinking bum, Mummy!

No I didn't! He's a liar.

Stop it! Both of you. Stop shouting!

Someone did stink, in fact. Someone − probably Ted − hadn't wiped themselves properly, and the smell of crusted, hours-old child shit floated around the car, getting in our noses, our hair, under our nails.

There was more yelling, then the desperate striking of arms too small to reach across the width of the car. In my mirror, I saw Paddy trying to squirm free of his seat belt, ducking under its restraints, reaching out an arm to meet his brother's, which were already flapping wildly in an attempt at defence.

We were driving down a long, quiet, residential street. There were no other cars in sight, no speed bumps, not even any pedestrians on the pavement. On a lamppost, a single bird shook its feathers, bent its head. I took one more look in the mirror, saw the boys making contact with each other now, squeaking with exertion, their outraged voices clear and high across the car. I could feel the rage rising, harshly familiar, a neglected friend. My nails dug into the density of the steering wheel, a pain grazing through my jaw as I clenched my teeth.

I put my foot on the accelerator and held it there, sensing the speed build in my chest, its force beginning to flatten me against my seat. As we sped up I could feel, rather than hear, the quiet taking over the back seat. Without looking, I could tell that Paddy was back in his belt now, looking straight ahead. Only when I got right to the end of the street did I lift my foot, slightly, begin to slow down. And only when I heard nothing for a number of seconds – only a smooth silence – did I check on them, seeing their faces watery and still in the mirror, neither returning to daydreams, or to fighting, but staring ahead, their eyes misted, unreadable.

~

She is a bad mother, *people might say.*

But: *Is a mother a human? they might ask. Or: only human-shaped, every limb in the right place?*

~

31

I met David Holmes in a restaurant I had never been to before: it had always seemed like a place you would have to dress up for, to wear the clothes widows wore in slick American dramas: tight dresses cinched in with a belt, sheer tights, patent leather stilettos. There was no occasion on which I could imagine booking this place: no birthday or anniversary that would make me seek its cream walls, the chic houseplants which covered its windows, making it impossible for passers-by to watch patrons eat.

David had specified the place and the time: I had left it open for this, for him to be in control. It had already seemed enough, to send it –

Okay. When? L

– in the middle of another sleepless night, the unslept hours like a black ocean around me, the bed a flimsy, rocking raft in the darkness. In the morning, I had to check that I had actually sent it, that I hadn't – as I'd done so many times before – simply stroked the message, left it in its place. I had never deleted it, liked to come back to it when my mind was particularly restless, when I feared my thoughts could burst from me, escape into the plain air beyond the window. They stilled me, these words: they made me pause.

He didn't reply for a number of hours. He had given up hoping, perhaps, regretted sending a message in the first place. Or he was just busy. Working. I tried to imagine him in a white lab coat, or in a busy lecture theatre, in front of a hundred students. But it was too difficult: he was only available in still frames, holding a glass of cheap faculty wine, taking a sip, making a small, polite expression of disapproval.

Now, I wondered if I would recognize him. I gave his name to the model-esque maître d', as though this was a business meeting. She held out a suited arm, gestured towards the back. Of course: he wouldn't sit close to the windows, even with the ferns for protection. Most likely, very few of the people he knew would come to a place like this either. They would have neighbourhood restaurants near their elegant, bay-windowed homes. They would know the waiters by name.

I saw him before he saw me: he seemed to be reading the menu with interest, and I wondered if he was going to choose some drippy, pungent brunch: eggs Florentine, perhaps, something I would have to watch slurping into his mouth. But as soon as I arrived at the table he put the menu to one side, firmly. He rose from his chair, gave me a closed-mouthed smile, a brisk handshake – the skin dry, cool – his eyes meeting mine before he sat back down. He looked more casual than I had seen him before, in a pale blue Oxford shirt, no jacket, the top button undone. He was older than I'd remembered; the skin on his neck was loose and drooping, his hands on the table lightly furred and covered with liver spots. He must have been at least ten years older than Vanessa. No wonder, I thought before I could stop myself, she had wanted Jake, his firmness, the still-boyish softness of his skin.

I looked down then, worried I was going red. I knew he was assessing me, the *wronged wife*. I had dressed in the best clothes I could find, but could feel my stomach inflating slowly over the brink of my trousers, my legs sinking too far into the leather of the chair.

It must seem strange – that I asked you here.

He said this without the tone of a question, as though he was completely sure of my feelings, that he had already assessed them, and found them reasonable. *Reasonable* was – I imagined – the highest goal of people like David and Vanessa Holmes, people with expansive bedrooms and tiny mortgages, who grew up believing it was reasonable to have the lives they wanted.

I nodded, sipped the water that was already poured at my place.

What did you want to see me about? I would not make small talk, I had decided: I would not put him at ease.

The waiter was coming over now – as David opened his mouth to speak he stopped himself, waited until I'd ordered, rearranged his hands on the table as I asked for tea. He still didn't appear nervous, only seemed to be taking the action that was appropriate in the moment. I had the sense that he would always know what to do, in any moment.

I actually— He cleared his throat; it was the same noise I'd heard on the phone. A protracted, liquid grunt. My stomach plunged, and recovered.

I actually have a request. A – well – a favour to ask.

I had my hand resting on my mouth, I realized, when his eyes flicked to it. I moved it down. I was barely aware of what my body was doing: it was the opposite of how he arranged himself, the slow way he made any change in his position. Perhaps, when he was younger, he had been more fluid, but I doubted it: I had met a few versions of his type at university, leftovers from an earlier age, men who knew exactly how to arrange themselves.

Right. I frowned, briefly: I couldn't help it.

The waiter came with my tea, checked whether David wanted anything – calling him *sir* – before returning to the front of the restaurant, the light from the windows that seemed faded, distant, as though it was already in the past.

I wanted to ask whether you could speak to your husband – he winced slightly when saying this last word, I noted – *about his work situation. About whether there was a possibility – a chance – that he might find* – another grunt – *employment. Elsewhere.*

Still, there was no questioning tone. It was closer to an order than a favour, I realized. This felt more like the identification of something I already knew than fresh knowledge: of course Professor David Holmes would never truly ask something of me, make himself vulnerable with a genuine request. He could, however, expect something from me.

This whole thing has been awful for my wife, you know – for Vanessa. The picture . . . I know she would never say anything. Would never ask . . . or you. But she's so happy there. And she didn't send it, so . . .

It was interesting, how anger appeared and disappeared in front of this man. How it dared to rise, tentatively, but – having nowhere to go, no possible expression – disappeared back inside me, was reabsorbed, seemed to be conveyed to my own hands instead, to their quaking, their inability to hold the dainty china cup without spilling my tea. I tried to keep my voice steady, at least.

Does Vanessa know you're here?

He shook his head quickly.

No. It would only upset her. She's been doing better – recently.

So you're staying together?

For the first time, I saw irritation present itself, before he could do anything to stop it: the smallest curve of his lip, an involuntary tightening of skin near his eye. His voice, when he spoke: just the lightest inflection of anger.

Well, yes. Of course. I believe in – he picked up a napkin, put it down, moved his leg; he was struggling, for a brief moment, to find the appropriate movement.

I believe in forgiveness. As do you, I presume? A nastiness now, unmistakable, his mouth and eyebrows moving at the same time. For a moment a wave of horror-heat threatened: did he know? I shook it away, visibly, my head moving; he couldn't know.

No? Well. That's interesting, definitely, but absolutely none of my business. His movements were exacting again, contained. *But, as I say, if you could suggest—*

I got up before I knew I was doing it: my chair fell to the ground with a loud crash, the noise breaking through the tinkling, ambient background of late morning. From the corner of my eye, I could see David Holmes reacting, or choosing not to. He was looking straight ahead, completely still, as though absorbing new knowledge, reaching an interesting conclusion.

He made no movement to help, did not call out my name. *It's a shame*, I could imagine him saying, shrugging his shoulders. *Sad for her.* Even when I was almost at the door of the restaurant, it seemed that I could see him, without turning my head, that I could watch the exact, smiling way he gestured the waiter over and asked for the bill.

~

A *piece of time, breakable, glass-transparent.*

I *watch her again: she walks away from the restaurant, moves down
the street. It is a bright day; she raises her hand to shade her eyes,
sees the light pass through her palm, jewelled red.*

The *world moves around her as it always does, a hive of unknown
lives. None of them noticing, none of them suspecting — even for a
second — what she has done.*

~

32

When the boys were babies, I often thought of going away. I imagined the seaside B&B I would book myself into, the way the light would come in the mornings, as though it didn't even notice that I was there. Objects themselves would be different, I imagined, kettles, pillows, shower heads, shoes: nothing would ask for my response. Nothing would need me.

I want a sunny day! Paddy wailed on the morning of his party. The day had started grey and cool, and I wondered what we had done to make him believe we could control the weather. Perhaps this was just one more party preparation I had forgotten to make. Did I have enough food choices for vegetarians? Had I planned enough games, or would there be some horrifying, gaping hole in the entertainment provision, as there had been at Paddy's sixth birthday? Fifteen tiny people staring at me from the middle of an empty wooden floor. Endless games of musical statues, until the older, cleverer children started to complain.

I spent the morning cleaning, tidying, making sandwiches in triangle shapes, cutting up dozens of carrot and cucumber batons that would not be eaten. It was important simply to have them displayed, to show that you were aware of the need to give children vegetables. I worked at a professional pace, my hands moving according to their own logic, slicing, arranging, decorating, blurred by speed, by the patterns they seemed to know instinctively, familiar shapes made in ease. I kept looking up – to see if anyone else would notice how fast I was, how accurate – but nobody did.

We had decided to have the party at home, to save money, but I had completely forgotten all the work this entailed, the large and growing gap between our house in its daily state and a house considered fit for public view. There would be twenty children there, including our own, a much higher number than I was expecting. Most people were not going away, it seemed; I had tried to sound happy when responding to every acceptance. *Wonderful*, I'd texted several times. *Paddy will be thrilled.*

Jake couldn't understand why I was going to so much effort: as with the Christmas party, he seemed reluctant to have it at all, seemed to want to keep our family a sealed unit, an airtight container.

You'll tell Paddy it's off then, will you? I'd challenged him, but he'd only shrugged.

I'm sure he'll love it. He had said this in a friendly way, as though my party-planning were a benign affliction, something that did good in the end. Ever since that afternoon in the upstairs hallway – our cheeks touching, my clothes pulled back – Jake seemed softened, placated: he no longer sighed loudly when he passed me, acted as if I was an obstruction in his way. On the morning itself, he helped, blowing up balloons, hanging a banner across the kitchen, hiding prizes for a treasure hunt.

A children's party, like a death, is never real until it is happening. It cannot truly be planned, or imagined. It is always unexpected. When the boys – they were all boys, despite my best efforts – burst in that day, I could see that, whatever my preparations, the party was going to be an ordeal. Or perhaps, I began to realize, it was *because* of my efforts, my stubborn insistence on adherence to the pirate theme, with all its associated weapons, the eye-patches that impeded each child's sight.

We opened the doors to the garden, watched them all tumble into the brightness – it was sunny now, unseasonably warm, and Paddy had thanked me for it – sword fighting on the grass, clambering onto the trampoline.

Shoes off! I shouted, putting the sound too much into my throat, so that it felt scraped, worn away. Jake stood at the doors with me, laughing at the sight of ten miniature pirates bouncing together, patches wobbling, swords pointing in the air. I watched him, amazed by the way he was able to find this funny rather than disturbing. I leaned into him, slightly, tried to absorb it by osmosis: this relaxed delight, the slight distance that seemed the key to enjoying parenting. I tried not to think of how much easier it was for *the husband* – the way family could be secondary, without excuses or apologies. We stood like that for two seconds, maybe three, soaking up the sunshine, its heat so like the warmth of love on our faces.

There was a broken scream from the trampoline, a stuttering yelp that turned to silence for a moment before erupting into a pure, baby-like cry. The children stopped bouncing abruptly, the netting sides settling back into place. And from the middle of them, two of the children – Paddy, and his friend Thomas – moved forwards. They were covered in blood.

It had been briefly exhilarating, to be given so many children to look after, when I knew I was barely capable of looking after two. As their parents left them – looking relieved, barely bothering to make small talk – I felt almost like confirming my credentials, my qualifications in child rearing. But I had none. I just smiled and tried to look competent, mature, motherly.

Now, with two injured children moving towards me, blood dripping from their noses, from their eyes, from their chins, I could see this was a mistake. I was no mother. I was a silly girl who had slipped and ended up in this kind of life. But I could play the role, as I always had. I rushed forwards, and Jake rushed forwards. I went towards Thomas first, looked at his face in the high sharp focus of panic. I could see straight away that there was one cut causing all the blood, maybe two inches across his forehead, a tear in the usual smoothness, an aberration. *He's okay.* This from Jake. *He has a nosebleed.*

I realized he was talking about Paddy, felt a rich rush of guilt at the way I had focused my attention on the other boy.

They must have bumped heads, or − I looked down at Paddy's hand, which held a small wooden sword.

That's not your sword, love, I said, realizing what must have happened. He'd borrowed someone else's, this strangely sharp thing, it must have jabbed Thomas by mistake − or on purpose − as they bounced. I prayed silently that it was an accident. *Please, please.*

I got a paper napkin, held it against Thomas's head. Outside, Jake ordered everyone off the trampoline. Paddy sat by my side, holding a wad of bloody tissue to his nose, taking a gulping sob every few seconds.

He hit me, Mummy, he gasped thickly through the blood − I looked down at Thomas, who shook his head unconvincingly, his eyes filling with tears. I felt a surge of joy: it wasn't my child, after all, who had committed an act of violence. It was this child, with his wholesome, ever-present at the school gates mother, his imposing, suit-wearing father. I smiled broadly before I could stop myself.

Well, no one should hit anyone, should they? I said blandly, making my mouth serious, trying to move my head equally between the two of them.

But, Mummy, I didn't! Paddy started to protest. *The sword hit him by accident, and then he punched me.* He was spluttering now, the blood from his nose still covering his teeth, his lips, spraying across the table as he spoke.

Put your head back, I told Paddy. *Anyway, let's just remember* – I did look at Thomas this time, I couldn't help it – *Kind hands, kind words. Isn't that what they say at school?* My pulse was returning to normal, at last. I tried to breathe slowly. It wasn't my fault, I kept trying to remember. I had given Paddy a good party; I had done everything I could.

I texted Thomas's mother, Sarah, as soon as it happened. It was important to be accountable, I knew that. To follow all the steps, as they did at school, where they sent home Accident Reports, strangely bureaucratic documents that featured a police murder-style outline of the human body, the injury a wobbly circle. *Hit shoulder on another child's head. Fell in the sensory garden. Applied ice.*

Thomas banged face while on the trampoline, I texted Sarah. *He okay, no stitches needed we think. X*

Was the mention of stitches reassuring, or not? Was a kiss inappropriate, or would the tone be too abrupt without one? I resisted the urge to apologize in the text, but when she arrived to collect him, the *sorries* poured out of me, liquid exhaustion, landing at her feet.

No problem, she said, tight lipped, inspecting Thomas's head. But then: *How many were on the trampoline?* She was looking straight through to the garden, where four or five boys, now weapon-free, bounced in the sunshine.

Well, there were quite a few, we took the swords away . . . I'm so sorry, Sarah, I really am. I feel terrible.

I did feel terrible, at that moment, even though Thomas's cut looked nearly healed already, his face glowing from playing musical bumps. He had eaten particularly well at the picnic, telling everyone loudly that he was a vegetarian, then eating five cheese sandwiches and a pile of raw vegetables. I told Sarah this, to make up for the injury. I was a good mother! I had chopped fucking carrots!

Sarah's face didn't change: she still looked at me as though she was my teacher, an infinitely more mature and discerning person. All of which was true. I had to say it.

Well, actually, he punched Paddy in the nose, so . . .

Her mouth pursed and I squirmed, tried to make light of it all. *Boys, eh?* – I couldn't stand it when people said this. It made me feel like screaming, like tearing my eyelashes out. And here I was, saying it.

Sarah raised her eyebrows. *Well, thanks for the party. Come on, Tommy.*

I held out Tommy's party bag, a final peace offering. The plastic was visibly heavy, well stocked, with tiny cartoon pirates climbing desperately up its sides. I could see Sarah pausing, but her son had already snatched the bag and begun to march out of the door, swinging it by its handle, humming quietly to himself. The other children left soon afterwards, a storm blowing through as quickly as it had arrived, leaving the house with a wrung-out quality, a palpable, damp atmosphere of relief. The four of us collapsed in the living room, the boys rooting in their goodies listlessly, Jake and I sighing, opening and closing our eyes.

He was sitting so close to me: suddenly, it seemed normal

to do this, to rest on his shoulder, to let my head fall gently against him. Jake leaned down and kissed the top of my head, briefly, my body still, not even flinching in response.

From the corner of my eye, I could see Ted watching silently, chewing a sweet, dribble beginning to appear at the side of his mouth. Paddy looked up too, after a moment, his attention briefly shifted from his party bag. I kept still, kept our bodies together, let the boys see us like this. *Happy.*

And maybe it could be real, this whole thing only a *blip*, something we'd talk about late at night, eventually, our words like dough stretching the past into different shapes, the darkness of our room making it all seem credible, necessary.

We would stop here, just as we had not conceived a third child, had realized in time that it would be a mistake. I put my head against Jake's chest, his heart a bumping road beneath my ear, a fractured process, contraction and relaxation, electric impulses that could stop at any time.

Two will be enough, I whispered against the fabric of his shirt, its floral-chemical wash filling my mouth, the sound of my voice barely loud enough for him to hear.

33

That night, we slept in the same bed, woke in the same bed. We turned to look at each other, breathed into each other's skin. These are things that married people do. It should not have been extraordinary. But it seemed years, not months, since I had seen this particular light on the speckled texture of his cheeks, his reddish stubble glinting up like embers.

I grew up knowing that falling in love was the most important thing I would ever do. Every song, every film confirmed it. But when Jake kissed me for the first time, I was surprised. I could describe it as something scientific, garden-like, botanical. A blooming, a stretching, my whole chest filled with clear air. Our kisses now – gentle, tentative – seemed laced with this moment, re-enactments of a distant history.

Jake took the children to their holiday club; he was meeting a colleague afterwards, someone he could discuss the investigation with, who would share rumours of its likely outcome. He'd shaved that morning, put on his smartest clothes. I watched him as he cajoled the boys, his shirt running smoothly to his belt. *My husband*. I felt a wave of pride, its contours unfamiliar, like something I hadn't felt for years.

•

When they'd gone, I turned to the remaining party mess, the banner attached to the wall, the strips of wrapping behind chairs. I started with the balloons, putting a few in the boys' room, gathering the rest for destruction. I held their bulbous bodies down – slightly slack, already – and made the stab with a pin, hearing the explosion, a surprise every time. I wondered, briefly, what the neighbours thought, whether it sounded like gunfire. In the reports from terrorist attacks, people never seemed to identify guns, at the beginning. Their first thoughts – and often their second, third, fourth thoughts – were of firecrackers, cars backfiring, the popping of balloons.

As I cleaned, time seemed to move incredibly slowly. I would look at the clock, do half a dozen things – put a packet in a cupboard, take the recycling out, pick a toy off the floor, pick five toys off the floor – and look at the clock again. I couldn't tell which had changed: me or time itself, if I was moving too fast for minutes to contain me as they used to. When I'd finished, there were still hours before I had to pick up the boys; I had time to myself.

I got ready, wore light clothes and shoes: I wanted to feel light, that my feet could lift easily from the ground. I took hardly anything with me, my hands were free: no one would know I had two children, dependent on me for everything. I walked past the field, to the meadows and river which ran behind it, turned my face to the grasses, my vision pulled to the horizon. There was a sweet, rich smell of sun on green, kayaks and swans passing by on the water. It was a moving, busy day; I turned my face to the wind, felt its smooth power against my skin.

I walked for a long time, passing student couples holding hands, talking quietly, toddlers scooting fatly past me on balance bikes, their feet skimming the ground. At last – tired, sweating

– I reached a pub on the other side of the meadows, a place
we often came with the boys at the weekends, bought them
cordial and soda water and crisps, enjoyed a few moments of
crunching peace, surrounded by other families doing the same.
It was quieter during the week. There were old men chatting
in groups, one smoothing his belly down in what looked like
pride, rocking on his stool, his pint floating golden in front of
him. A couple about to begin their meal, the woman with her
knife and fork hovering above her plate, inspecting each chip
before she ate them. A number of empty tables. I would order
lunch, I decided, perhaps sit in the garden. I walked towards
the back, where the space narrowed, became Victorian and
twisting, a series of abrupt turns, dead-end corners.

They were there. Jake and Vanessa. Sitting on opposite sides
of a table, having lunch. Vanessa had almost finished: her lasagne
was streaked messily across her plate, a piece of salad dangled
from her fork. I was looking at that when Jake saw me, jumped
from the table. I kept focusing on the green stripe, disappearing
into her mouth.

*Lucy! What are you—? V – Vanessa – we were just talking about
the hearing. The investigation, I mean.*

I didn't want – couldn't – see his face, see the way his
expressions would change, the quality of his gaze as he lied. I
left fast, bumping into people: one woman spilled her drink,
shouted out to me. I half-ran back over the meadows, his words
beating through my steps.

We

were

just

talking

We

were

just

talking

It might have been the truth. But why had he lied this morning, his face so close to mine? I was sure Jake had used the word *he* to describe the colleague, could hear the word repeated now, mocking me. And why had they chosen that pub? It was barely out of town, although away from the most dense university bustle. *Safe mid-week*, they must have assumed.

Vanessa had only turned around briefly, but I'd seen her expression. There was no remorse in it, I thought, only a blank kind of non-recognition, as though she'd never seen me before. The river, previously a melting, soothing length, was now disturbed by the wind, a coolly rushing water, Vanessa's look running through it.

The trees blew in my face. My T-shirt stuck under my arms, was damp at my neck. A pain radiated from my chest; my heart was burning, it seemed, turning pink-orange like a saint's on a statue. It was dripping, I could imagine, seeping into me.

I got home, kicked my shoes off in the hallway. There was still an hour before I had to get the boys from school. I walked up and down, pressed my hands into my eyes, dug my nails into my skin. These hands: they'd always looked gentle to me, small and soft, almost like a child's hands, more densely patterned the closer I looked. But now they looked different, larger somehow, the nails too long and curving. Not a writer's hands, or an academic's hands, as it turned out. Something else.

I left the house again, slamming the door, not checking – as I usually did – to see if it was locked. I walked towards the shops: I'd made myself a list, some things I would need. Along the pavement, across the sky, I saw the rest of the day laid out in front of me: how *pleasant* I would be, how helpful and composed with the boys, with their squabbles and pains.

I would go to my room when they were occupied, with television or each other. I would look out of the window, across the field, at the trees in their perfect lines, unchanging, the kind of witnesses I needed, signs that I was still alive.

It is the last time. He lies down, a warm night, his T-shirt pulled up, his head turned away.

•

The first cut doesn't seem to be enough. Jake continues lying still, his eyes closed peacefully, as though he hasn't felt anything.

I lift a piece of tissue and catch the drop of blood that is rolling down his leg, towards the bed, the white sheets. It spreads out across the thin paper, a circle, a red eye.

Okay? This seems a stupid question, even as I am saying it. It is exactly what the anaesthetist said to me, as the surgeon split my body apart.

But Jake nods, clearly, without opening his eyes. I take this as permission, as an invitation to continue. Surely, if it was over, he would sit up, would show me it was finished. But he does none of this. He stays, continues to be still.

•

It isn't a razor for shaving your legs. It doesn't have a plastic coating, a moisturizing strip. It is a *straight*, a *cut-throat*, an implement

Jake has barely used. A fad, an Internet purchase abandoned almost at once.

It has a wooden handle, curved and smooth as a boat. A shimmering, five-inch blade. *Eco-friendly*, he told me. There were videos, he said, where men shaved successfully with it, day after day, flicking the blade in the light.

I remembered the way he'd practised with it one autumn afternoon, how we'd both winced as he cut his skin once, and again, the blood travelling in single drops, individuals landing in the sink.

•

He agreed to it as soon as he came home, his whole body defeated.

One last time. The third: the one that should make all the difference.

Do your worst, Lu. A slow, sliding movement of his mouth, the imitation of a smile. He looked at the ground, at his own fingers. He didn't look at me.

I could still smell beer on his breath, couldn't stop seeing Vanessa's back, the piece of lettuce on her fork. Other details had emerged slowly, over the hours.

As I bought the disinfectant, I'd seen an expression – Vanessa's – the same one I'd seen at the Christmas party, something between pity and a sneer.

As I'd put the boys to bed, I could see her skirt, under the table. Leather, I thought. And her boots: patent, knee-high, a stout heel.

Her legs crossed. The architectural outline of her neck, the groove of her bra strap.

Her feet: were they tangled with Jake's? However hard I tried, I couldn't see.

•

It was Jake's idea to do it on his thigh. A flickering unreality, as he took off his trousers, pulled up the leg of his boxers.

I felt the power I had always witnessed in reverse: doctors, nurses, midwives, hovering over my body. Free to do as they wanted. The seconds before they made their move, a masked intimacy, a blurred lack of recognition.

I always closed my eyes, as Jake does. I never wanted to see.

•

The blade presses harder. But. Something has gone wrong; instead of a drop, it is a swell. It is a wall, a wave, a tide. *My fault.*

Instead of silence, there is screaming, coming from neither and both of us, surrounding our heads, his body, my hands, floating out of the window, towards the sun.

34

At first, I tried to stem the bleeding myself. I pressed wads of toilet paper against the cut, but the blood was coming too fast. Jake was calling out, looking down, telling me to try something, then something else.

How hard did you press? he said at one moment, his eyes wide and slightly unsteady, as though they might roll back in his head.

I said nothing; there was nothing I could say. The moment I had cut him was lost to me, blacked out. It seemed irrelevant now, anyway; nothing was relevant but the blood, the fact that it wouldn't stop. *You knew this would happen,* a voice in my head was saying, over and over again. *You did it deliberately.*

Shut up. I shouted out loud, turning as though to spit something out.

What? Jake was panicking, moving too much.

I'll have to call an ambulance, I said, my voice steadier now, the old pink pyjamas I was holding against him turning maroon, blossoming out and out, endless, colours behind closed eyelids. Jake was pale, his skin glossy and bare, like new paint.

A wave of nausea. I looked down, retched into my cupped hand. *An accident. It was an accident.*

The woman on the phone seemed angry with me. *She knows,* I couldn't help thinking. *Somehow, she knows everything.* She kept asking me questions: was he breathing? Was he bleeding from the eyes? All the questions were about Jake, about his body; none of them were about what had happened. *An accident*, I'd said, at the beginning of the call. *An accident with a razor.* Nothing else seemed to be needed.

It'll be there in five minutes, she said, eventually, in her strange, plain voice. *Make sure the door is open. Make sure the paramedics can enter the premises.*

I nodded, pointlessly, put the phone down on the bed.

I looked at my hands, lifted them to my face, felt the rough lack of comfort in my own touch. I had done it all, but what had I done? I could feel the flight of my own mind fluttering within my skull, hitting bone as it tried to escape.

I tried to think of something normal to say. *Unbelievable!* Surely we'd laugh about this, later on, in a few weeks, a few years. Wouldn't we? But Jake's eyes were closed again; not peacefully this time: they were screwed tight, creased shut in agony.

~

Here: the third time. There is no going back now.

Never before has she had blood like this. Under her nails. Under her tongue, somehow. From her fingers to her mouth.

However much she spits and drinks, it will not go away. She had forgotten what it tastes like: a hot pavement, a forearm, fresh from the swimming pool. Like a birth room: like the future.

~

35

If we pulled the curtains all the way around, there was privacy. There was a rectangle of it, the bed, the drip with its hanging bag, the chair for me to sit in. Jake's parents were still with the children, as they'd been since last night, summoned by a phone call, by a brief, false explanation. Jake was due to be released the next day; there was anaesthetic, fears of infection, a staggering number of stitches.

He was on a high floor, in the bed closest to the window. While Jake slept, exhausted by pain and medication, I stared out of the window, over the bland fields where work had begun on another wing of the hospital, cranes and diggers bright and stark against the wash of the sky. The last times – the only times – we had been in hospital together before this, our children were being born. Time didn't move in hospital, I had noticed back then: it pooled, gathered, got stuck.

The one time my mother was hospitalized, we didn't know it was happening. *She's having her wisdom teeth out*, we were told, and for years – decades – afterwards I thought this was what dental surgery did to your face, that it caused swollen lumps around the eyes and mouth, that it somehow painted the colours of a storm – deep indigo, bottle green, streaks of navy – across the cheeks.

Children can suspend their disbelief to an extraordinary degree, I was told later. Things that make absolutely no sense – the neck cast, *the wrist cast* – can become plausible, can be blended into the picture, be made to fit. It was a different hospital to this one, but it looked just the same. Same floor, same windows as those I stood at now – thick, plastic, jump-proof – looking out at clouds moving across the day.

Now, the curtains moved, awkwardly, as though someone wanted to knock. The sound of a man clearing his throat.

Mrs Stevenson? A voice, so clear and authoritative. The curtains parted. A white coat, a pale, thin face. The doctor asked whether, despite Jake's apparent *lack of history*, there was something going on they should know about.

Does he ever talk about hurting himself? Has he ever attempted suicide? I answered no to everything, kept my eyes down. I knew he was trained to spot people like me: liars, sadists. Monsters. My hands curled over in my pockets, the nails sharp against my palms. I had wiped the razor, buried it without thinking in our household bin, under teabags and banana skins, the waste of our week.

At any moment, I thought, I would be dragged away: I kept picturing the men who would take me, a criminal-looking gang with masks over their faces, pulling me out of the high clear light of the hospital, recoiling in revulsion as they fastened my handcuffs.

The doctor asked his questions, and I answered them, my mouth dry and twisting, my voice coming out high, then low.

I went into the room, and he had the razor. There was blood everywhere . . .

The whole time we spoke, Jake slept beside us, his breath falling gently in and out of his mouth, dreaming as though nothing was wrong. Various hospital staff walked past, some turning their heads to stare through the open curtains. At one point, two nurses walked past together; I saw the look they gave me, the way they turned back to see one more time.

The guilt — if this was what it was — lay on my back like an animal, a physical sensation of heaviness. I stared at the hospital floor, the shining squares of it, crawling with invisible disease. This was abuse, wasn't it? It was *domestic violence*. I deserved the looks, and so much more. What Jake did wasn't a crime. I almost told the doctor the truth. I wanted to be taken away, suddenly, to be led into whatever punishment they would give. But he wasn't accusing me of anything. He was saying something else.

Thank you, Mrs Stevenson. I understand this must be very hard. Mrs Stevenson?

Mrs Stevenson raised her head. A woman on a hospital ward talking to a doctor raised her head, and nodded. She thanked him — Dr Davies. She looked away, so she didn't have to shake his hand. She felt the curtains at her back, looked at her husband — Mr Stevenson — lying in bed, his curls sinking into the pillow, his face colourless. She stared out of the window again, at the miles and miles of sky, stretching into an unknown horizon. The cars leaving the car park, their red lights shining like something new. Teams of swallows flying to the next field, the next tree; they were just practising, Paddy had told her once. They were just getting ready, preparing their wings for months of continuous flight.

~

She still thinks she knows what she is doing. She will go home, she imagines, and she will make food for her children, for her in-laws.

She will smile and clean and soothe. She will make it all okay.

~

36

I stepped out of the hospital, squinted in the light. My head was air-filled, flying into the world around me, the car park, the shuffling patients in flapping gowns, the buildings that loomed and shifted above me.

I walked a few yards: my body felt clumsy, enormous, the weight on my back even heavier. I knew I needed to move, to travel faster, escape the slowness of foot against pavement. I called a taxi, rested my head against its window, gave the driver my address without opening my eyes. I'd had a text from my mother-in-law, knew everyone was at the park, would be there for hours still, the boys licking ice creams and gliding down slides, oblivious.

At the house, the empty rooms looked at me as though I was a stranger. The sun passed through, blocks of shine on the walls. A blue vase, a wedding present, photos in silver frames: a family, smiling. Magazines, shoes, letters, decks of playing cards. Every object seemed to have its own mind, the stuffed dinosaur forlorn, a stack of dishes in the sink accusing. It had been wrong, I saw now, to get attached to this place, just a building, one I didn't even own. I wrestled my bike out of the side alley, pedalled down the street as though it was a normal day, into nothing, having no idea where I was going.

I had always loved cycling, the wheels turning under me, as easy as walking should be, idling gently or speeding, feeling almost airborne. Years ago, before leaving my PhD, I had spent whole days doing rings of another, similar town, going from common land to common land, contemplating lying under a cow, rolling in mud. Anything seemed better than going back to the library. I had been feeling my motivation ebbing, had noticed a hope, rather than a fear, that I would fall pregnant, that I could push all those books away.

Now, I realized I was ravenous, the huge hunger still there, despite it all, an engine working without thought, consuming everything. I went to a burger place, ordered a supersized meal, sat in a booth where my legs stuck to the seats. The eating worked, as it had before, all thought blotted out by sensation, by chewing, the morphing of solid objects into a flood of taste and swallow, salt swept down by fizz, meat giving its oils to my fingers.

But when I finished, my stomach taut, the thinking came back: David Holmes, his grey eyebrows moving upwards:

I believe in forgiveness. As do you, I presume?

To forgive is divine, I was taught growing up. So when I first saw my father slap my mother across the face, I decided to forgive him. I closed my eyes and prayed to God to help me, to pour his quiet pastel lights over the image in my mind, the continual replay, the way she fell. And within hours, I noticed my feelings towards my father change. When he asked how I was, I stopped scowling and turning away. I started saying, *Fine, thanks.* I had forgiven him, it seemed, God had helped me; it was done.

But little by little, I noticed another feeling growing inside me. The image of my mother – on the carpet, crying – was not gone, I realized, but transformed. My anger had been diluted, bleached into a pale trace of its form, a covert operator that I would continually – for months, for years – mistake for something else.

~

In primary school: a boy who fancied me. Who would push me against the brick walls, pretend it was a game, a joke.

Once, he kicked me hard in the stomach. A corner of the playground, a dip in the brick. From the edge of the sky: a single wing tip, slicing into view.

My first kiss: a boy called Mike held his arm in front of a door, told me I couldn't go back inside until I did it. The inside of his mouth was a watery cave, a place I thought I might never escape.

Somewhere at the back, near his throat: a clawed shape, moving towards me.

~

37

When I left the burger place, it was still light outside, the sky electric blue at its peak, softening as it curved, flattened itself against the town. I sat on a bench by the river, watched the water travelling beyond me, the ducks passively moved along its surface. When a rowing boat sliced past – the cox screaming through a microphone – I turned my head away. I waited until it was clear: no boats, no people. Just water, waiting.

I looked at the phone in my hands, my nails hooked around it. I lifted my arm and threw: such a small gesture, one second, less. A tiny moment, something that could be blanked out later. The razor. Pressing harder. The phone through the air, landing in the water, sinking quickly, easily. Gone.

I glanced around, to see if anyone was watching. Was this a crime? Throwing my phone away? Polluting the river. When I was a child, I was terrified I would accidentally steal things, that I would put things in my bag without realizing. I imagined the moment of discovery, the way I would be guilty, without even knowing it, without even trying.

If my dad caught me being naughty, there would be slaps on the backs of my legs, nothing major, the same as my friends had. The worst thing, by far, was her face. My mother's disappointment was an energy source: it could power a whole country.

I'm sorry, Mama, I used to say, going to lie on my bed, the sting on my thighs the best thing I had – sharp, clear – the voices starting up their old routine. *Disgusting girl. Stupid idiot.*

She would tell me to pray to God whenever I got angry. To help me become a better person. *My good girl.* She liked me to be next to her at the altar, for us to lift our hands for the wafer together, our knees close on the velvet.

I always looked at the priest in that moment, had the worst thought I could manage. The pendulum of his cock and balls, swinging like a bell under his robes. The distant crusted cavities of his nose, the slimed alien of his tongue. I thought of pressing the wafer back into *his* throat, the way his eyes would round in surprise. I was never my mother's good girl.

I tried my fucking best. I realized I had said that out loud, glanced around to check if anyone had heard. There was no one: only trees, the city light hazing their leaves in a peached glow. Then: a single swan gliding downstream, the arc of her neck a question mark, the soft curve of her feathers like a *yes* on the water.

~

The first harpies I saw were almost faceless, their eyes pale slits, their hair thick black lines, flying in shapes behind their heads.

Like my hair, I used to say as a child, touching the page, the hair, the skeletal wings.

No, my mother said, frowning, moving my hand away. Not like you at all.

~

38

As I cycled closer to the centre of town, I saw groups of people out for the night, dressed for the heat in short-sleeved shirts, tiny dresses. It was Friday, I realized; I couldn't remember when this had last meant something to me. I thought of the first proper party I went to, the lapis blue halter-neck dress I wore, no bra. I remembered kissing fifteen boys that night, their hands on my waist, the way the whole thing went from excitement to self-reproach so fluidly, hardly a gap at all.

You did what? my mother said, when I'd told her some of it. *You little slut! One boy at a time!*

I'd cowered, felt the rot creeping up my legs, another word to add to my litany. *Slut.* She'd laughed then, offered me an arm. *Silly girl.* She'd kissed the top of my head.

As I cycled, I tried to stay beside trees, close to buildings, turning my head away. It was possible, I had begun to realize, that Jake had told the truth now, that people were looking for me. My face could be on the Internet, on posters. *Vicious assault on husband.* But I was relieved to discover, as I passed groups of people, couples, students, drunk men in tight shirts, that I was as invisible as ever.

Elderly women are said to be invisible, but I found that it happened much earlier than that: I blamed motherhood, the stains on my clothes, the darkness of fatigue under my eyes, my head down, hurrying. Of course, women will always look, will notice the way your jeans are slightly too tight, the good colour of your hair. But now the men looked away. Even when I stopped under a group of builders working late, there were no calls, no whistles. They played their loud music, and they laughed, possibly at me. They laughed and let their legs hang down, not even looking at how far they could fall.

I curved over the handlebars, lifted my shoulders, pedalled away. When I was a teenager, I almost developed a hunchback from trying to hide my breasts. From trying not to let anyone see.

Stand up straight, my father would say. But I saw what happened if I did that. When I ordered drinks in a cafe, in a bar, men stared directly at my chest, as though ordering from me. At a certain point, I lost weight – *tits on a stick*, boys in my class laughed – and every time I left the house men called to me; they followed me home. I watched them in every shop, every street, every library. Grown men, old men, holding their wives' hands, staring at me, running their eyes up and down, taking me in.

One night I left a club alone after a fight with a friend, staggered to find my own taxi. In the morning I woke up aching inside. No wallet, no phone. Nothing left but bruises, a sourness that seemed to have become my whole body. *A blackout.* The darkness was full of holes, I discovered, tiny memories that seeped out, one by one. A sharp smell, a turn of a head. Fingers at my hips, against my throat. *My fault.*

~

For a long time, I used to lie in bed and pray to the harpy to get the ones who hurt me, to punish them, scratch their faces, their hands.

I imagined their surprise when they saw her: a shadow growing, taking shape in the air.

~

39

It started to seem that I had been cycling forever, my body drenched in itself, my limbs molten with exertion, still pushing me on. I was on a long, ugly road now, lined with exiled supermarkets, car garages, strings of grey-edged houses ringed by the traffic. At its end, I knew, was a tiny, crouched chapel built for lepers a thousand years ago. I wondered if it would be open, if I could lie down on the pews, be blessed by something that might feel like God. There would be silence, the strange, continuous hum of my mind, the odd harmony that I knew underlay everything, if you listened carefully enough.

But I was afraid, still, of things worse than me: ghosts and killers, beer-breathed men in the dark. Even now, I thought someone would want me, or want to kill me; this seemed to be the same thing. I cycled straight past the chapel, looping back towards the scented, still world of the university town at night, patched with grassland, bridges, the ancient buildings that were meant to be beautiful.

I reached the river again: the world was beginning to blur, to merge into an undifferentiated mass, a prehistory whirl of plants, birds, the occasional, dizzying burst of sky. The water lurched beside me, leathery black, welcoming. I followed its bends, a thick ribbon that pulled me with it, on and on, until it veered away and I rejoined the endless flood of cars, hearing radios, phone calls home, talk of dinner and *back soon*.

I kept going this time, even when the road went over a motorway, layered bridges shocked by the thunder of heavy goods trucks. Concrete and metal and – somewhere, far away – the sky. This was the gouged dividing line, the place where house prices dropped, pristine medieval ornaments giving way to simple geometry: the flat line of a field of wheat, the squared-off rolling of clouds. The cars passed me too close, indifferent to the way their wing mirrors came within inches of my handlebars. I kept pushing, kept moving, the hedges breaking at intervals to reveal the full evening light across the landscape, its deep yellow pinking at the edges, smoked by fumes.

I went through one village, and another, my legs raw with fatigue now, bruised-feeling, overripe fruit before it drops to the ground. I considered cycling even further, until I reached the sea, perhaps, some two hundred miles. I would pedal until my wheels got stuck in the sand, until I had to lie the bike down on its side, lie beside it, let the beach be shaped by my body.

But I was not going to the ocean: I was moving towards a still and familiar point, back to what I knew. The next village was an opening of memory, framed images of lost life. The school gates, mute and mysterious in the dusk, the patch of green, darkened by tall trees, where I'd swigged neat vodka, its taste brutal against the leaves. A small shop, a church bell tower in the distance, and I was there: the turning that became too familiar, over the years, its reoccurrence only disappointment, by the time I left. But now it was something else: a sagging, collapsed version of itself, a picture of time.

I was unsure, at first, if this was even the same house: I did not remember its window-eyes sinking towards the door like that, the grimace of its defeat, as though embarrassed, unwilling to look at me. A farmer had rented it to my parents cheaply, and since they'd left a series of even worse tenants – or squatters – had made their mark, scored a burn above the kitchen, a scrawl of graffiti across the door.

It didn't take much pushing: the locks were old and rotten, loosened by those who'd been there before me. They had left themselves scattered: beer cans, a single shoe, the sea-creature curls of abandoned condoms. My parents had always rented – like me – always managed to find places with problems. This one, the place we stayed longest, had mould and damp even when we lived there, and now it covered every wall, a deep black-green reaching beyond itself, to the garden and beyond, places where there were no other walls for miles.

When they first viewed the house, my mother said it appealed to them, to be on their own. *Detached*. No one listening. And the garden: an acre of it, a tamed patch, the wildness at its edges always trying to get through, my mother and father fighting it with seed packets, weedkiller, a common enemy. The house itself was always cracking and dark at the corners, but my mother tried to keep it nice: she scrubbed and fussed, just as I had fussed and scrubbed. And my father *helped*, just like Jake, and he fucked other women, just as my husband had.

I'd heard them screaming about it, right in this room, could, if I squinted, see their voices moving across the walls, as clear as the mould, a palimpsest of their presence. When he finally left, just before I did, what struck me most was the silence: the way my mother and I, together, made almost no sound. For years, I would forget that she had died – suddenly, her heart simply *giving up* one afternoon – would want to ask her questions, ask her opinion, create noise to replace the time when we didn't speak.

The last I knew of my father, he'd left the country, gone somewhere sweet and hot. It made sense to me, that he had run away to that place, where people's lives seemed to swim with pleasure: good food, clear light, beautiful bodies. He would never have to return to this dampness, see the garden as it was now, a jungle at the windows.

I trailed through the rooms, looking for things I knew I would never find: old toys, my best picture book. I looked for the place where I had scratched my name, below the window-sill, but found only faded white paint, a blank silence. Underneath the quiet, I could feel the people who had been here after us, shifting traces of their unknown lives.

There was a mattress in the corner of the room, a scrappy old blanket. I lay down on my side, feeling my back settle as I did, my mind now filling every pore of my skin, starting a gentle fire, the tip of a candle along my arms, my legs, my shoulders. I was drained, entirely exhausted, but this surface was flaring, flocking into the edges of myself, the places where I touched the mattress, the points where I ended and the world began.

There was still some light at the window: the last of this day, weak and indifferent. There was no one wanting me, nothing to do. There was the window, asking nothing. The door, simply itself, no needs, no loud voice. The sound of my heartbeat, the feel of my limbs against the blanket. My skin, warm and restless. I began to take my clothes off, piece by piece, thinking of the dirty mattress as I did it, other sensations stronger, more important.

I ran the brittle, cracked cusps of my fingernails up and down my skin, pure, unspeakable relief. It was the feeling of rare foreign holidays as a child, covered in mosquito bites that my mother told me not to scratch, the unleashed bliss of finally letting myself do it, of sensation meeting its answer in my own hand. I thought of the scratch mitts that the boys had had to wear as newborns, the way that Ted's face looked, the one time I was too busy to remember to put them on. Covered in his own scratches, red lines across his chin, his cheeks, his forehead. *My baby*, I had moaned. He'd looked ruined, at that moment. *I've let it happen*, I'd told myself. Should have stopped him, somehow.

I got up, as though I would leave, get back on my bike, ride through the night to their skins, their sweet breath on mine. But it was completely dark now: the windows showed me nothing. I sank to my knees, closed my eyes, seeing lights in the corners of my vision, hearing a roaring in my ears, a rush like the wind passing over the tops of trees. I moved my nails into my hair, hunched over, the weight on my back like two hands, pressing me down.

Then: it seems, for a moment, that none of it has happened. That I am at home, and my babies are with me. I am daydreaming, it seems, soaring now above church spires, building sites, playgrounds. I can see every detail, the stitching on clothes drying in gardens, the words on their labels. I can go on, glide over the sea, over boats, islands, towards an ever-shifting horizon, only distance, no time: only *this*.

I open my eyes, grasping at myself, certain I will see something: creatures, scabs, appearing, growing. I look and look, searching my own body, every inch of it. There is nothing there.

~

But in the middle of the night I do see, and laugh: it is happening now, as I always knew it would.

I am her: I am here.

~

IV

~

I wake up with the feeling that I am being watched. I open my eyes and see the wall, the window still as a waiting animal, looking for me.

The glass is broken, its crack a pattern, a message. I have given up trying to read it.

~

I have been here for weeks, I think. Or: for a single day, the longest I have ever known. There has been knocking, and I have ignored it. More than this: I hid.

I found a hiding place where I could keep telling it — my story, her story. The way we ended up.

~

A truck moves past on the main road, so heavy that the floor shakes. But it is far away: it won't come here.

I *roll onto my side, lift my neck. Somewhere behind me, my back lays out its separate pains, a rustling complaint. I lie back down.*

~

This daylight is not enough: I want more, the strongest I can find, the danger of bright sunshine.

I sit up, careful with myself – a memory of something, post-surgery – but this time, instead of being cut, my body is one. My breasts meet my stomach, my stomach meets my legs.

They greet each other, as though bowing, and I see it now: the way clothes kept everything apart.

~

I manage to stand, my feet light on the ground, curled nails touching the slip-shine of biscuit wrappers, crisp packets. I lower my head to the floor and taste them, taking out the last crumbs with my tongue.

~

I think that walls don't matter as much any more. I hold myself on the edge of the window, savour the new morning airs. Soil: meat and burning. Grass: mint-cool.

I open my mouth wide: I can keep it like this now, I realize. No one will tell me to close it.

~

There are so many greens, each one like a face, like a body lying down in pleasure. Neon, lime, emerald, sage and teal and jade.

There is the field, the wood. These are my places now.

~

A shout from somewhere, far into the village. A young voice, high and wanting. A certain feeling with this, a pain or a touch, but it seems that all feelings are the same.

She – I – wasted so much time trying to tell the difference.

~

The stairs now, missing the gaps where holes invite me in, my body easier, getting used to it. I go to the garden, one movement, not stamping the air down like I used to. Letting it carry me.

Every cloud is clearing, I can see. I can see so much. If I close my eyes, there is a map of everything, the whole world laid out, piece by piece. I could move myself towards it. But I will stay. Look down at myself. This is enough.

~

The way it feels to grow again: a shooting across the heart, like a rock falling from space, dissolving between my bones.

I could make a study of myself, show it to everyone. Say who was right and who was wrong. Which writer-man said I would be *repulsive, dressed in rags – I am dressed in nothing! – or seated on a throne.*

~

It seems to be the afternoon: the sun is lower again and I believe this means afternoon. Bells somewhere nearby, chiming.

I lie across the stubble grass of the field, feeling the burn of some distant planet turn my skin red and hard. Then I realize: I could be seen. From a plane or a drone or another secret way.

I move, merge with the shadows, the undergrowth, the world a warm body beneath me.

~

Something hard in the grass, wooden, smelling of decay, of the life that fills its splits. A tassel of frayed rope: a swing, I think.

I watch a woodlouse crawl across rot, try to imagine the seat as it used to be, gliding into the sky.

~

I go towards the trees: it is night. I am crawling now, can feel my stomach brushing against the grass. Tiger belly, low, furred, being touched by the earth.

The greenness moves into me – the wet, the pathways, my hands in soil, the grass longer now, across my neck. It seeks my mouth.

The dark is not as thick as I would like: it is pattered by light, grazed and smashed by it.

Here, I think gravity will let me go at last. I will fall upwards and onwards: I will drop into the stars.

~

I am hungry, I suspect. It is more complicated now. I listen. How many different kinds of hunger there are: scraping, whining, reaching.

A thousand sensations, I see now, not just one.

~

I think my new hands will be good for picking berries, and they are; some are low enough for me to close my teeth straight onto, others make me stand and pluck, my mouth sour-sweet with their coldness.

I lean against a stump, rest my head against my shoulder. I am not cold, although I should be, and I am not afraid, which is the best thing, the night a glowing darkness ahead of me, trees shifting in the gloom.

I can hide in my own body now. I can close my eyes.

~

I am woken by a bear, I think, or an earthquake. Something that takes the early morning and snaps it in two. There was before the noise – full belly, soft rest – and afterwards, a threat that looms, giant, over everything.

An engine. This is what it is, I realize, an engine not on the far-away road but much closer. Outside the house.

Fear now, for the first time, clearer than anything else, a cool light that moves through me. I have to get away.

~

I am close to the house in only a few movements, almost weightless now, able to leap huge distances, as in dreams, excitement and terror a single thing. My head moves from side to side, seeing everything. Every leaf on every tree, moving like a chorus, a glistening crowd.

I know how to sneak around the corner so I am not seen, how to get to the road without any eyes on me. But something goes wrong. There are voices calling a name in the new day, this strain of a day, barely got going. It is too early: it is too soon.

They can't see me – not like this.

The thought moves through my mind, whispered quietly, as though by someone else.

~

I have to keep going, reach the road. I feel the weight on my back slowing me down. But my heart is beating faster than I have ever felt it before: it is a single sensation now, a hum, firing up, getting ready.

I open my mouth, to let something out. The sound is sharp, biting, a ripping blare. I do it again.

~

The engine is starting again now, it might be faster even than me. There is no time to get beyond, only this place, a church, a tower, bells that ring out. There are steps, easy for me, the engine stopping outside, the voices. I am above them, my breath coming ragged, in scraps.

At the top, a door with a sign, a warning. I open it, open a path right onto the day. The whole village is laid out, just as I see it in my mind. The streets, the motorway, the creeping start of the town.

I can see it all: the way I thought I would live. The people I spent my days with.

Somewhere out there: her house. My house. Paddy. Ted. Jake.

~

There are shouts downstairs, steps getting closer.

And here: I am gripping the edge of the stone.

I *crouch. Pull my head in, look around. I move to the very edge, keeping my eyes fixed on the distance.*

I *look towards the light.*

I *take off.*

Thank You

To the brilliant women who nurtured and helped to shape this book meticulously at every stage: my agent, Emma Paterson, and editors Charlie Greig, Sophie Jonathan, Katie Raissian and Elisabeth Schmitz. Team Harpy: what incredible luck to work with you all.

To Camilla Elworthy, Lucy Scholes, Paul Baggaley, John Mark Boling, Deb Seager, Morgan Entrekin, Lisa Baker, Lesley Thorne, Anna Watkins and all at Picador, Grove Atlantic and Aitken Alexander who've shown such faith in my writing.

To earliest readers and cherished friends: Rebecca Sollom and Kaddy Benyon. To a (shed) builder of the highest order: Nicholas Sabey. To my parents, Penny and Ernie, for their constant kindness and encouragement.

Finally, to my husband and children, who do not feature in this book and yet helped me to write it in endless ways. With huge love and gratitude: Tim, Leo, Sylvie.